INTO THE SPIRAL

Charles Ashton has lived most of his life in Scotland and recently moved back to the village where he was brought up. His books for young people include The Dragon Fire Trilogy, *Jet Smoke and Dragon Fire* (shortlisted for both the Guardian Fiction Award and the W H Smith Mind Boggling Books Award), *Into The Spiral* and *The Shining Bridge,* as well as another novel, *Billy's Drift,* and two stories for younger readers *Ruth and The Blue Horse* and *The Giant's Boot* (shortlisted for the 1995 Smarties Book Prize). "Why do I write?" he says. "Well, why do I start to go to pieces after a year or two of doing anything else? If I have to 'go out' and look for a job now, the first thing I shall have to tell my prospective employer is that I am unreliable – take me on at your own risk." He is married with five children and a variety of animals.

Also by Charles Ashton

INTO
THE SPIRAL

CHARLES ASHTON

WALKER BOOKS
AND SUBSIDIARIES
LONDON • BOSTON • SYDNEY

First published 1992 by Walker Books Ltd
87 Vauxhall Walk, London SE11 5HJ

This edition published 1996

2 4 6 8 10 9 7 5 3 1

Printed in England

British Library Cataloguing in Publication Data
A catalogue record for this book is available
from the British Library.

ISBN 0-7445-4742-3

For Anna

CONTENTS

1

FRUSTRATION

The chill dusk of a spring evening filled the village square with a dreamy, violet light. Everything looked wet, dark and distinct – the bare linden trees, the carved rams' heads on the gable ends of the village hall, the low grey houses on the other side of the square with their purple slates or chocolate-brown thatch. The air was almost misty, and there was a scent of wet earth mixed with the scent of wood-smoke from the chimneys.

In the bare garden of one of the houses two women were talking. A large lady in a hat decorated with artificial fruit was towering over a small thin one standing on the doorstep. The small thin one nodded towards something across the square, and the large one turned to watch a girl and a boy who had just come out from under the lindens and were making their way up the side of the hall away from the square. The girl, who was a little taller than the boy, had curly hair the colour that the roof-thatch would turn in the summer, and the boy had a large black crow perched on his shoulder.

The two women watched the boy and the girl until they were out of sight. Then the large woman turned to the thin one and looked down her nose and said, "Talking to crows that come and perch on his shoulder! There's something not at all right about that boy."

The smaller woman sniffed, like a weasel coming up out of its burrow. "His father was a queer one too," she remarked.

"And look what happened to him," said the large one, who was called Ms Redwall and who had the whitest lace curtains in Copperhill. "Not a Trader, but just as bad as a Trader." Her head, and the imitation fruit, nodded twice. "Not a trace of him left, all those years ago, and poor Ms Overton left with a baby to bring up all by herself."

"Little wonder he talks to crows now," said the smaller woman, and sniffed again.

"That's where it starts," said Ms Redwall, "but what will it be next?"

"What sort of ideas is he putting into that young girl's head, that's another thing," said the small woman.

"That is another matter altogether," said Ms

Redwall, and pursed her lips. "I gather *she* has enough queer ideas of her own – and I should know, because she's friends with poor Ms Clodish's daughter next door."

"What sort of ideas?"

Ms Redwall's mouth pursed even more, and the imitation fruit nodded several more times. "Ideas," she murmured, "about – other places, if you know what I mean."

The small woman obviously did know what she meant, and looked suitably shocked. "Whoever heard of a young thing like that in charge of the school, anyway?" she said.

"Something ought to be done about it," said Ms Redwall, and looked thoughtful.

After a few more minutes of talk Ms Redwall and her fruit parted from the small woman, who disappeared into her house and shut the door. Presently there was no one to be seen in the square and the grey dusk deepened, helped along by a mist that rolled down from the great cloudy mountain towering above the roof-tops.

The boy and the girl meanwhile were making their way up a steep cobbled road that led out of the village under a line of tall ragged elms. Into one of these trees the crow had just flapped up in a rather clumsy fashion and the boy was rubbing his shoulder where the bird's claws had been digging into him.

"Good night, Herold!" he called in answer to the squawk that came down from among a tangle of bare branches. Then he said to the girl, "He's – really, he's just not like a bird. I can't explain it."

"You're imagining things," the girl, Kittel, said firmly. "It's getting to you at last. You're getting confused – probably going mad. Poor Sparrow."

Sparrow ignored her. "He's not sort of – flighty, like other birds," he said. "He's not like other crows either. Crows are always sort of ashamed of themselves. Herold's not. Maybe he doesn't have to be, because he doesn't eat the sort of things other crows eat."

"With the amount of food you give him to eat," Kittel retorted, "he ought to be the sleekest and glossiest crow ever. Instead he's the most awful flying mess anyone's ever seen. So maybe you're right after all. Maybe he became a bird by mistake."

"Do you think so?" Sparrow said with a frown.

"I was joking, stupid," said Kittel.

The mist became thicker as they climbed, and the chill of the air was a reminder that the mountain above them was still half covered with snow. The last part of their journey was up a steep, winding path, whose white pebbles shone in the gathering gloom. Quite suddenly they were at the top of the hill and looking down to a long, whitewashed cottage, whose lights made a golden halo in the mist. The door was open, letting the light stream out from the hallway.

Sparrow stopped just before they went in. "I'm going to tell Murie tonight," he said.

In the year and a bit since Kittel had so unexpectedly come to live with them, Murie, Sparrow's mother, had become extremely fond of her. Murie had always wanted a daughter of her own. She knew that, one day, Kittel would probably have to try to find a way back to her own home, which was a mysterious and dangerous-sounding place somewhere away beyond the mountains. But as nobody even knew how far the mountains stretched, it seemed like the sort of thing you could always put off till next year, or even the year after. They had thought to begin with that people from Kittel's place would come to look for her, but there had been no sign of them.

"It's because of the wall of mist," Sparrow said. But, as the months went by, it seemed that the wall of mist was fading away, and still no one came, and Kittel became more and more settled in her new home with Murie and Sparrow.

"My roof worked," Sparrow announced, as the three of them sat dipping bread into their broth at the large table in the lamp-lit kitchen.

Murie, bread dripping in her hand, looked up and looked blank, as she often did with Sparrow. "What roof?"

"On the cottage. In Kittel's valley," Sparrow said with his mouth full.

Murie continued to look blank.

"I told you about the cottage, back last year. Remember? I was asking if my father could have built it and you said I was talking nonsense."

"Oh, that cottage," Murie said, with deliberate calmness. She was noticing an excited expression in Sparrow's eyes. "Don't run your fingers through your hair, it'll get all full of soup and bread."

"I went back to it yesterday and it's as dry as anything inside."

Murie picked her spoon up and took two mouthfuls of soup before saying, "Are you telling me you want to be a thatcher, or what?"

Sparrow glanced at Kittel, but Kittel was examining her bread carefully, pulling out the small black seeds in it and eating them separately.

"Kittel and me are going—"

"Kittel and *I*," Kittel murmured.

– "to try and find the way back to her home. We're going to start from the cottage . . ."

Murie put down her spoon again. "You're

14

going to start from the cottage," she repeated. She knew quite well what Sparrow was saying, but she was determined not to understand.

"We can spend the night in the cottage, and start off from it in the morning."

A deep silence fell, a silence made somehow deeper by the gentle bubbling of the large iron pot on the fire. Even Kittel, who came from a different place, knew Sparrow had said something awful.

"I've been out at night before," Sparrow said at last, when the silence seemed to have gone on long enough.

"That was different," Murie snapped. "You were with what's-his-name."

There was another silence.

"People don't stay out at night," said Murie finally.

"We wouldn't *be* out!" Sparrow exclaimed. "There's a door, and now there's a roof! It's a real house!"

"It's out in the middle of nowhere," Murie said firmly. "Miles and miles out into the mountains."

"Someone must have lived there once," Sparrow argued.

"Well, they're not there now – so what happened to them?"

"Traders are out at night," Sparrow said, though he knew by now he had lost the argument.

"Traders are different," his mother said. "Traders take their life in their hands. Look what happened to Bull's father."

Sparrow sighed.

Murie got up from the table and turned to the black cooking range that crouched by the wall under the huge clay oven. She started slamming the embers about with a poker and throwing fresh logs in. "What does Kittel think about this?" she demanded. "Do you want to find your way home?"

"Well – there's the school," Kittel murmured, "and Lissie, and – other things . . . No . . . Yes . . . I don't know." She was not often at such a loss. Her misty blue eyes looked mistier than usual. "I like it here, you know," she finished lamely.

Sparrow looked offended.

"But I do think we should try to find a way home," she added hastily.

"I see what it is," Murie said, jamming a last log in under the black pot. "Sparrow wants to go exploring, so's persuaded Kittel out on this wild-goose chase too."

"I don't! It's not that!" Sparrow protested.

Murie started ladling out more broth. "Right," she said, "I'll tell you what. We'll leave it for just now. The nights are too dark, and the weather's not good enough at the moment. When the spring gets going, there'll be a lot of work to do. After that, say

16

at the beginning of summer, the nights will be brighter; and then perhaps – *perhaps* – I'll let you go for a couple of days: as long as you don't get into any scrapes in the meantime."

The spring came on. Mist came and went on the mountain above the village and the dark patches grew bigger on its snowy upper slopes. The tender crocus spears pushed up in the flowerbed in front of the house; snow came, flattened them, and melted the next day. Daffodils began to make yellow masses amongst the tired yellow grass, and birds began to sing amongst the budding trees. Kittel watched it all rather wistfully, Sparrow impatiently.

Gogs Westward and his father came over with their team of horses to break the ploughed ground in Murie's steep little fields, and Sparrow and Kittel went up and down behind them, scattering corn, then up and down behind them again, poking in the grains of corn the rake hadn't covered. There was digging, sowing, planting and weeding to do in the vegetable garden, and everyone had to lend a hand. Whenever they finished a job on their own land, they went over to Bull Hind's house on the next hillock and helped Bull and his grandmother on theirs, and sometimes on to the next to help with Gogs', though Gogs' family was big enough not to need much help.

The days grew longer, the sun climbed higher

above the mountains day by day. The handsome black cockerel would make sure no one stayed in their beds after four o'clock in the morning.

"Any day now . . ." Sparrow was muttering to himself one May morning as he climbed up through the heavy-scented gorse towards where the forest began at the top edge of their fields. "She's got to – she's got to – if we don't go now we'll never go . . ." He wasn't saying it to anyone in particular and he got no answer back, except that there was a lark high above his head, trilling something that sounded like "easy easy easy does it, easy does it, easy does it," which Sparrow found faintly irritating.

As he climbed, he kept glancing round, stumbling and hurrying on. Just learn to be patient, Murie had said the night before, but already he was beginning to feel that the summer was ticking away. Kittel seemed to be losing all the interest she had had in his plan and spent most of her free time out of school with her friend Lissie. Perhaps it wasn't surprising, since the last time she had seen the cottage it was just four damp walls and no roof and certainly didn't look inviting as a place to live in. It wasn't his fault that she hadn't seen it with its amazing roof on, its shutters of woven twigs, log chairs and pile of sticks stored ready for burning in the huge fireplace.

An elder tree leaned over the wall that bounded

the top edge of the field, its bony trunk pushing the stones out of place so that it was easy to climb over. Sparrow hauled himself up by the yielding branches and stood on top of the wall, scanning first the fields below him and then the sky above him. Then all at once he sprang up off the wall, looking to begin with as though he were going to jump back into the field. . .

Except that he didn't come down, but rose higher into the air: flying, not jumping. He hung for a moment above the field, and then with an effortless twist of his body rose over the elder and disappeared into the glistening green canopy of the beech tree that overhung it.

High among the lattice of the tree's silver branches he paused and landed, straddling a slim bough and peering down, around, and up towards the blue sky mottled among the topmost leaves. Then he smiled, straightened, and seemed about to launch himself upwards again – when suddenly his expression changed, he slumped limply back on his branch and heaved a deep sigh.

Directly above him, perched half hidden in a thicket of leaves, was the crow, Herold. Herold was the most marvellously untidy bird Sparrow had ever met, with hardly a feather that wasn't askew or moth-eaten looking, but for all that, he had an uncanny knack of knowing exactly where Sparrow was going to be at any time of the day or night. Faint churring noises were coming from his beak now, which was what had caught Sparrow's attention, and one black eye was glaring stonily down at him. Sparrow sighed again.

The churring noise changed to a series of soft squeaks and rasps, then the beak snapped shut.

"To the cottage," Sparrow said tiredly, in answer. "I wanted to try and go a bit further today." He glanced down at a squirrel, which had suddenly gone scampering like a russet whiplash down the trunk of the tree. He smiled slightly as he watched it dive into a drift of dead leaves on the ground far below and gaze back up at them, bewildered.

But the crow was squeaking and rasping again, and this time there was an edge to the sound which was just a little threatening. Sparrow stopped smiling. "Of course I haven't had enough of you, Herold," he said pleadingly. "You're fine. You're wonderful. Honestly. It's just you can't – I mean, I can fly faster by myself. You get tired, flying there, and back; you won't manage to go further."

At that the crow seemed to explode, hopping off its perch and sending a flurry of leaves and feathers round Sparrow as it flapped furiously and let out a torrent of squawks and screeches. Sparrow covered his head and closed his eyes, and didn't open them again until the noise had died down and the crow had resettled itself on two twigs, with its legs straight out and rather far apart, looking very much the way people do when they stand with their hands on their hips.

Sparrow was quite used to the crow's rages, and had an excellent reason for covering his head, but he also knew they never lasted long. After a few moments he said, "So what about Kittel? She can't come with us if we do it your way, you know that."

The crow made several more, rather quieter noises, at which Sparrow snorted, "Of course she can't walk. There's forests and rough ground and boulders and bogs. She'd take days getting there."

Herold clicked and clacked his beak and squeaked several times. Sparrow sighed a third time.

"Oh, all right," he said at last. "But she'd be a lot more interested if she could come and see for herself. Come on then."

A moment later the crow had flapped itself clear of the treetop and was wheeling in its odd, lopsided fashion over the green masses of forest on the lower slopes of the large mountain. Of Sparrow there was no sign, either amongst the trees or in the air.

2

THE LINDEN LADY

If Ms Redwall had known the full truth about Sparrow, her concern would have become deep shock. For her, the idea of his having a pet crow was bad enough. If she had known that it was not a pet at all but a wild bird, and that it sat on Sparrow's shoulder because Sparrow could understand the speech of beasts and birds, her disapproval would have changed to horrified amazement. If she had known that the crow had first started speaking to Sparrow because it had seen Sparrow flying, she would probably have had a seizure – which certainly would have saved everyone a lot of trouble.

However, Sparrow kept his remarkable gifts a close secret from all but a small circle of people – his best friends Gogs and

Bull, Bull's grandmother, Murie, Kittel and Kittel's friend Lissie (who lived next door to Ms Redwall). Apart from that, there were only rumours – hints dropped by Kittel in the classroom; strange things Sparrow said or did which couldn't be accounted for; and memories of the startling events of eighteen months before, when Kittel had suddenly appeared in Copperhill village after being rescued by Sparrow from a crashed aeroplane on a mountain-top. It was these things which made some of the ordinary village people whisper and wonder and shake their heads; but none of them knew enough to make any reasonable guesses, and the truth wouldn't have occurred to them even in their wildest dreams.

Apart from being able to fly and understanding the language of beasts and birds, Sparrow had one other gift, possibly the greatest and strangest of the three. As the crow flapped steadily onwards through valley and over ridge and among the tall mountains, it was this third gift that Sparrow was using: he was in the crow's shape.

This was why he was not seeing the world quite as he usually saw it: in crow-shape he could view all at once the ground speeding below him, the great arch of sky above him, and the sunlight and shadow of the hillsides on either side. The only direction – apart from behind – in which he found it difficult to see was straight ahead. He had to make his crow-eyes roll together if he wanted to do that – as you have to do if you want to focus on the end of your nose – or else turn his head first to one side and then to the other. A crow isn't normally thinking about getting anywhere in particular, and its eyes are more made for searching for food and keeping out of trouble.

In fact, after the interest of it had worn off, it was a bit of a nuisance flying in the crow's shape – part of the nuisance that life had become since Herold had befriended Sparrow the previous autumn. Sparrow hadn't been able to use his gift of flight properly for months now, because Herold refused absolutely to let him; every time he tried to, the crow was there to stop it. Herold did this mainly by reminding him of all the help the birds had given in building the roof on the cottage, and saying that if friendship meant anything at all, Sparrow should let himself be saved from the obscenity of being a flying boy. He should leave the flying to the birds.

It was afternoon by the time Sparrow wheeled over the last ridge and glided down into Kittel's valley, and his crow-shape felt tired. In a way this didn't matter, because after perching in a pine tree and dropping down to the ground in his own boy-shape, Sparrow didn't feel tired at all. Herold felt as though he'd just woken up from a long sleep – that was what it was like for him when Sparrow was in his shape.

Kittel's valley or, as she called it, "the Valley of Murmuring Water, like in a Chinese fairy-tale", was a secret, remote place far beyond the furthest limits that the people of Copperhill ever travelled to. How the cottage had got there Sparrow couldn't begin to guess, which was why he had vaguely wondered if it could have been built by his lost father.

If you stood outside and looked around, you felt you were in the bottom of a deep bowl, on whose edges rough heathery ground gathered into sheer, rocky cliffs as the mountains towered up all round. Down a long cleft in one of the cliffs a thin white waterfall poured, filling the bowl with a constant soft noise as though the mountains were gently breathing. But where the water ran across the floor of the valley it was in a deep, dark channel, and there it made hardly any sound except for the occasional swirl and *ploop* when a trout hit the surface. Kittel had given the valley its name when Sparrow first flew there with her in the autumn.

The cottage certainly looked different now from the way it had looked then. Not everyone would have said it looked better. Herold and his army of birds – Herold had grown up amongst them, though he looked down on them now that he lived in Copperhill – had been most interested in Sparrow's idea of getting a roof on. They had put a huge amount of time and energy into building the "great, upside-down nest" which the boy wanted.

For that was how it came out. A real thatcher wouldn't have recognized that it was a roof; he would just have seen an untidy mound of twigs and leaves and dead grass heaped like a haystack on the roof-timbers of the ruined cottage. Yet it proved thick and dense enough to keep out the roughest winter weather.

Ignoring Herold's complaining croon from the pine tree, Sparrow walked down to the cottage. He wandered round it, as he always did when he arrived in the little valley, and sighed. It wasn't much use without Kittel.

The queerest thing about it – apart from its new roof – was its doorway. It was an extraordinary doorway to find on such a tiny building. Its two massive stone doorposts were not upright but, when looked at from the front, leant out to the sides. Over them, the two lintel-stones were set together to form a point over the centre. Into this five-sided space there fitted a massive five-sided door.

After a while, there seemed nothing more to check about the cottage, and Sparrow stood by the door and gazed off eastward where the stream took its way out of the valley. The afternoon sun was shining full on a rocky ridge cut by a sharp, dark, gully. If he went in crow's shape, that was the way he would have to take. If he flew himself, a single bound would take him high above the ridge and into sight of the lands beyond. He had seen these from a distance but had never followed the stream. Following the stream was the course he and Kittel had agreed would be best, as long as it went eastwards – eastwards was the direction of the old railway line before it got lost in the mountains not far out of Copperhill. They knew the railway line had once, long ago, linked the village with Kittel's place.

Murie was right, of course. Sparrow wanted Kittel there as his reason for going on, but it was really for himself that he wanted to find the way to her place. He was hungry to see the incredible world she had described to him so often – televisions full of colours and people talking, lights that made a whole room bright just by touching a thing on a wall, traffic roaring, crowds of people rushing through the bright-lit streets, people who didn't know you, people you'd never seen before. He wasn't sure if he would feel safe to go there without Kittel to guide him: on the other hand, just a glimpse might be safe enough . . . if he could get there

27

quick enough . . . if he flew by himself. . .

A loud squawk behind him put a stop to his thoughts. Herold always knew: always. It was like having a nanny looking after you, never letting you alone, never letting you grow up. Sparrow bit his lip, and his eyes prickled with frustration.

He took a deep breath and nodded towards the ridge.

"That's the way we'll have to go," he said.

Herold complained that the sun was hot enough to frazzle his feathers.

"You don't have to come," Sparrow said.

That set the crow off into a rage again and it started half flapping, half running, round and round the roof, screaming the sort of abuse that crows scream at each other in their more excited moments. To save it from exhausting itself, Sparrow took its shape again, picked himself up from the somersault down the roof which the sudden shape-change caused, and set off at a glide for the gully, skimming over the bright grass of the valley and the fragrant birch forest at the eastern end.

When Sparrow insisted to Kittel that Herold was different from other birds, it was because of a faint feeling of difference he had every time he took the crow's shape. It was hard to say exactly what it was. Normally, with birds he changed into, he felt that his bones were full of air: birds were so light they hardly seemed to belong to the ground at all. It was as if the crow somehow felt its own weight a little bit — a tiny bit — more than other birds. It was like the ghost of an old sadness. Sparrow wondered if it was simply connected with Herold's being so fond of sleeping. He didn't believe Herold was a very old crow, though he did think he was probably very lazy. Whatever the feeling was, he never got entirely used to it — either that, or it was getting stronger.

The effect of the gully on his crow-vision was dramatic. The rocky walls drew suddenly, blackly, in, like a lid slamming on either side of his head. The sunlight was cut off. The echo of the water battled to and fro and grew to a monotonous drumming, a dizzying noise that swirled round the small black thing he was, wrapping him in cocoons of sound. Sparrow could almost see the sound, spinning away like a tunnel ahead of him — a black tunnel, stretching on and on, flecked with flashes of silver that were the continuous boom-boom-boom of the drum. . .

He was not flying any more. He was walking, in his own shape, down that black and silver tunnel, dreamily, vaguely, stumbling as though he were walking in his sleep. He couldn't think what had happened to Herold, though that didn't seem to matter. He almost let his eyes close as he stumbled on down, down, down. . .

A cool, laughing voice cut across Sparrow's dulled senses: "You were going a dangerous way – you're lucky I was here to find you!" He stopped, wrenching his eyes wide open, blinking stupidly.

He was no longer in the black and silver tunnel, but in what seemed to be a wide, low-roofed chamber with walls of bluish stuff like ice or frosted glass. The walls let light through but no glimpse of anything outside. Sparrow hardly noticed this, for he was staring, goggle-eyed, at the lady who had so unexpectedly interrupted his strange journey.

Sparrow had seen plenty of girls and women before, but never anyone he could exactly have called a lady. This person was. You could see she had never done a stroke of work in her life, had never been out in burning sun or cutting wind or chapping frost. She was very beautiful, with long reddish hair that looked as though each strand had been polished a thousand times. Her skin was smooth and pale as ivory. Her dress was green, covered with a jungle of designs in gold thread.

"Come," she said, smiling, "you must be hungry after coming so far."

Sparrow frowned. He had not remembered being hungry; but now, as the lady spoke, he realized that he felt ravenous. He felt as if he hadn't eaten for a week. His stomach seemed like a gaping hole that would need a barrow-load of food to fill it.

"Yes, I am," he said, puzzled.

He let the lady take his hand. The touch of her fine, long-nailed fingers was soft and cool as water in a sun-warmed pool. Round her there hung a faint scent like the smell of linden blossom, and he fell again into a strange dreaminess. They crossed under a low archway in the bluish wall, and there in front of them, in a second chamber like the first, was a great table of glass, laden from end to end with the most tremendous feast Sparrow had ever seen.

The dishes, bowls, trenchers, pitchers and platters seemed too many to count, and each was filled with something that looked delicious. There were pastries and pâtés, roast fowl and fondues, fruit and fish and a great fat-oozing pig's head with an apple stuck in its mouth. Sparrow's stomach seemed to be howling with agony, and his mouth watered so much he couldn't speak. He had never felt such hunger.

"Eat – whatever you like," the lady said, delicately picking up a piece of succulent skewered meat and sinking her crystal-white teeth into it.

It was too much for Sparrow. He felt his sides were caving in for want of food. He rounded on the glass table, ready to seize whatever was nearest . . .

But he stopped, his hand poised above the plate from which the lady had eaten. A pickled

31

eel in a yellow sauce on a nearby dish had moved. In fact, it was crawling. It slithered off the plate and across the table, winding between the dishes; and as it passed under Sparrow's hand it raised its yellow-streaked, pickled head and spoke. "First, the stone in your pocket," it said.

Sparrow, although stunned, became quite clear-headed. It was true that he had his stone in his pocket – or in the pouch that hung from his belt, to be exact. He always kept it with him, in case he got the chance to hand it back to old Puckel. Puckel was the only person who would be able to turn the stone back into the mountain it really was. It was Puckel who, a year and a half before, had given Sparrow his magical powers.

He glanced at the lady. It seemed she had not noticed the talking eel. He picked up a piece of skewered meat like the lady's, but at the same time he drew the stone out of his pouch.

He was immediately seized by a giddy feeling of being hurled backwards very fast; yet nothing moved. The bluish, translucent walls became like clouds which seemed to shift slightly, so that he could see through them glimpses of the way he had come, the stony gully. The lady was changing in front of his eyes, withering, drooping, her hair falling away from the front of her head, leaving her a big bald dome of forehead, and something strange was happening to her arms. Sparrow went on clutching the stone, gritting his teeth against the awful feeing of falling backwards. He still seemed to be clutching the skewer of meat, too, but when he glanced down, he saw it was Herold he was holding.

And now the lady had become a shadowy figure in a straggly grey cloak, an ungainly humped thing that shuffled along over stony ground. The feeling of violent movement lessened, and Sparrow saw a second, then a third, figure exactly like her: deep-shaded humps of grey cloak, no faces visible. They were shuffling slowly, and now Sparrow could see that they were on the shore of a still water, where swirls of deep mist made it difficult to make out anything clearly. They were moving away from him and paid him no attention. If it were really the lady he was seeing, she seemed to have lost all interest in him.

"I don't understand," Sparrow said aloud. He looked down at the crow in his hand. Herold was as motionless as a stuffed bird.

With a ripple and a swish, the waters of the lakeside parted, and Sparrow found the black, beady eyes of an otter fixed on him. The animal's glistening wet fur was black as jet, but for a strange streak of vivid yellow-gold across one side of its face. It was a very unusual-looking otter, but seemed real and solid compared with the deep-cloaked figures receding into the mist. The otter brushed a paw across its whiskers. Sparrow heard it say, "What you don't understand is pretty much."

There was something about the creature which made Sparrow think immediately of the eel. The same sinuous, winding way of moving, the same sound to the voice. "What on earth's going on?" he demanded, and heard the otter reply, as it brushed its other paw forward across its face –

"Not on earth, but under earth, through water, and by the Secret Way of the Mountains."

Sparrow saw that the animal's eyes had a queer, slightly glazed look – more than a little like the eyes of the pickled eel. It turned its blunt muzzle side-on to him and arched its back. Then he heard its voice – which somehow didn't sound as though it quite belonged to it: "There they go – see? This is the moving of a stone from where it should be to where it shouldn't be. And that puts everything out." The otter gazed after the three figures, almost out of sight now in the swirling mist. Then it turned away towards the water. "Puckel must know this quickly," it added. "That stone will take you. Under the Pole Star, only then." With a soft ripple it disappeared.

The mist seemed to be drawing back from the water and from the stony shore. Silently, uncannily, it grew clear.

The light was dim. Sparrow found himself in the twilight of evening beside the shore of a long, pale-shining lake with tangled trees growing all along its edges. Through their trunks soft clouds of mist went creeping. Seized by sudden panic, he gathered himself and leaped into the air.

High above the shimmering silver of the water's face, he paused, hovered, and looked down. The lake spread eastwards for what looked like several miles. But westwards, there was a rocky defile where a stream that fed the lake flowed through. He flew a little higher — and there, over the far end of the defile, he saw the little valley he had left that afternoon: his own valley, with the cottage and its heaped-up roof.

Holding the still body of the crow against his chest, Sparrow sped homewards.

3

RETURN TO COPPERHILL

In the dusk of that same evening Kittel sat by the Cold Stone, waiting. The lights were twinkling in the valley below and the Old Road was a pale band, glimmering between rock walls and low bushes off up into the mountains.

The only sounds were the occasional calling of a lamb from down in the fields round the village or the call of a curlew somewhere above; and all the time there was the soft, restless tinkle of water falling into the stone trough at the Cold Stone's foot.

Kittel was waiting for her friend, Lissie Clodish, who was coming back with her father from the next village. Lissie had been staying in Villas for the last three days. A visit by one of the young people of Copperhill to one of the other villages was something which had not happened before. This one had come about after a terrible row between Lissie's mother and father about his work as a Trader, and it was all being kept very secret.

"There are four other villages in the Mountains," Kittel announced one day to her class in school, to gasps of disbelief. "Sparrow has been to them all."

"What are they like? What are they like?" came from all sides of the schoolroom.

"They're just like ours. They're not very interesting," Sparrow assured them. But it made no difference — now everyone wanted to see them. It was a far bigger sensation than when Kittel had spoken about astronomy and people having been on the moon.

The only problem was the parents. No one's parents would talk about the other villages, or even admit they existed. A couple of boys were beaten for mentioning them. One girl was stopped from coming to school altogether.

As a Trader, Lissie's father, Don Clodish, regularly made journeys to Villas, Drakewater, and even Springing Wood and Uplands, bringing back glass and scythes and salt in exchange for the copper pans and distilling vats which were made in Copperhill. But no one would talk about the Traders either. Lissie's mother simply pretended she didn't know what her husband did for a living.

"It's so silly!" Kittel laughed. "I just can't believe it. It's like long ago, when they wouldn't believe the earth was round."

"I know," Lissie said, hanging her head. "But you can't do anything about it."

"They're all mad," said Kittel scornfully.

"You'll have to be careful, Kittel," said Lissie. "People are starting to talk about you. I can't talk about school with my mum any more. I'm sure there's going to be trouble."

"Stupid," Kittel snorted.

The dim cloppity-clop-clop of hoofs echoed down towards her from a distant bend. In a while the dark shapes of two horses appeared and came slowly down the road.

"Whoa! I almost missed you there, Kittel," came Don Clodish's voice. "Had you fallen asleep?"

Kittel got up and smiled. Lissie scrambled down from in front of him on the leading horse. "The poem first!" she said, holding up her finger.

Cut in the stone of the little water trough were the words:

> Take of my water
> Enough for your need;
> Then onward, true-hearted,
> I bid you good-speed.

Before Kittel had arrived in Copperhill, no one had been able to read the words at the base of the Cold Stone; now Lissie made a point of reading them aloud whenever she passed. Lissie was fond of rhymes.

"Hello, Kittel," she said when she had finished. Her eyes were shining in the dark.

"What was it like?" Kittel said.

Lissie sighed. "It was wonderful – oh, I just can't tell you what it was like... There was this boy ... and there was the dog, Boffin, and a house all covered with yellow roses, and a ruin in the garden – I want us to move and live there – and great oak forests, and the garden's really big and there's a pool with these enormous holly trees – it's called the Hollywell – and Ormand's mum doesn't bother about anything and – did I tell you there was this boy called Ormand...?" She broke off and sighed again.

They walked along behind the two tall horses, all misshapen in the twilight with their bags and bundles. The road came down to the apple orchards on the edge of the village, then climbed again past the foot of the three round hillocks of Overton.

They parted there, and Kittel climbed on up the path to the house on the top of the nearest hill. In the kitchen, Murie was bad-temperedly washing dishes. She was bad tempered because she was worrying about Sparrow not being home and she had broken a plate as a result.

But Kittel had barely begun to help her when Sparrow ran into the house with his hair wild and his eyes wide.

Murie rounded on him. "Where have you been?" she demanded. "I've been worried to death!"

"He – He – Herold – " Sparrow panted in return, ignoring her question. "Something's happened to him!"

Murie looked with distaste at the ragged bundle of feathers in Sparrow's hands. She didn't care much for crows, however interesting and intelligent Sparrow might claim they were. "He looks all right to me," she said. "As cheeky as ever, anyway."

"What?" said Sparrow in surprise, and held his dark handful up to the light. Herold's eye winked at him maliciously. "Herold!" he exclaimed. "I thought you were dead!"

The great beak snapped a few times and the eye rolled anxiously in Murie's direction. Herold was convinced that Murie had murder in her eyes.

Sparrow hurried out – not that he really thought Murie would try to murder Herold – and Kittel followed him, anxious to hear what had happened. Murie, grumbling to herself, returned to the sink. She didn't really want to know where Sparrow had been; she found his doings too dizzying anyway, and the main thing was that he was back.

Kittel was just in time to see Sparrow release the crow, who flew up to the nearest treetop, squawking with indignation. Sparrow told Kittel of his strange adventure in the gully, and the message he had been given by the otter; but long before they had got anywhere near understanding what it was all about, Murie called to Sparrow that he might at least come and eat the supper she'd made, even if he didn't intend telling her where he'd been.

The next day there was school. Lissie wasn't there; and Sparrow fidgeted and couldn't settle to anything. A couple of times Kittel told him to get out if he wasn't going to take part. He didn't go.

School was definitely not what it used to be. It couldn't be, when the teacher was no older than the older pupils. To start with, when she had first become the teacher over a year before, Kittel had tried Ms Minn's old method of standing up in front of the class and telling them things. It was Lissie who had changed all that. Lissie was a great mimic, as well as liking rhymes. (She could do Ms Redwall's turned-up nose, pushed-out bottom and snooty voice quite beautifully.) One day she had got up in the class and done such a perfect imitation of Kittel's teacher-ish, rather bossy, manner that everyone was soon rolling about in helpless laughter. Kittel had been a little offended, but things had become a good deal more relaxed after that, and Kittel and Lissie became close friends.

When Lissie had done her famous Kittel-imitation, she had spoken a little nonsense rhyme, which went:

> Honey is sour and vinegar's sweet
> If I were a cow I'd never eat meat;
> A wheel is square and a brick is round
> If I were a fish I'd never get drowned.

Everyone loved it. "Go on, do some more," they urged her, and Lissie added another rhyme that came into her head:

> So when you're sorry and want some fun
> Fling a bucket of water up to the sun,
> Then all join hands, with winks and grins
> And shout like mad when the rain begins!

There was an uproar of delight. The two rhymes were put together, a tune was found for them, and "Lissie's Song" became the basis for a wet and rowdy playground game.

So far, no one had interfered with the youngsters at school. Most of the parents were grateful to Kittel for taking their little ones off their hands now that old Ms Minn had gone. But Lissie was right – there were murmurings. Ms Redwall seemed to be constantly hanging round the school these days, though she always made it look as though she had just stopped for a chat with someone or other. Not long after she had first decided that "something ought to be done" about Kittel, she had persuaded her sister to remove her son – Gogs – from the school. It was "not nice", she said, for the lad to be taught by a girl of his own age, especially when dear Ms Minn had been taken from them so tragically. Next on her list was her neighbour, Lissie's mother, who, thanks to Ms Redwall, now firmly believed that Kittel was trying to turn the children against their parents.

"Why does she always have to be around?" said Bull as he left the school with Sparrow and Kittel at the end of the day. He stared rudely at Ms Redwall as they passed her, turning his head to go on staring behind him as they went on up the road. As Bull had piercing blue eyes and frowning black brows, a stare from him was quite impressive, and Ms Redwall was left flushing and muttering about the manners of the school children now that they didn't have a real teacher. Bull laughed. "My gran says that if there was a prize for stupidity she'd even come ahead of the donkeys," he said.

Bull's house was on the middle one of the three rounded hillocks which the village people called Overton: there was Overton itself, where Sparrow and Kittel lived, then Hind – Bull's home – then Westward, which was where Ms

Redwall's sister lived. Bull always went home with Sparrow and Kittel. When they were out of the village and under the row of elms where Herold spent most of his time, Sparrow began to tell Bull about his strange experience of the day before. Bull was a good person to turn to when you had a problem: he listened carefully and thought deeply, and even if he couldn't come up with a new way of looking at the problem himself, he could go and get his grandmother's advice. And that was normally the best advice you could get anywhere in the village.

As if to back up Sparrow's story, Herold came fluttering down from his tree like an old leaf in a storm. In fact his flying was so bad today he did a complete somersault before landing half on, half off Sparrow's shoulder.

Sparrow waited patiently as the crow scrabbled back into position beside his ear. "What's wrong?" he said. "Why are you flying so queerly?"

The crow rasped and rattled in reply.

"Where's it gone?" Sparrow asked.

"What's he saying? Where's what gone?" Kittel broke in impatiently.

"His trailing edge," said Sparrow. "He says it's missing."

"His wha — ?" Kittel was beginning, when Herold burst into a fresh series of excited squeaks and clicks, and stretched one of his wings out in front of Sparrow's eyes. Sparrow had to grab hold of it to stop the crow toppling off again. Then he stared. "Look at that," he said.

There was a half-moon of feathers missing from the edge of the wing. From the look of them, they could only have been chewed off. In his mind's eye, Sparrow saw the pearly teeth of the linden lady sinking into the piece of meat. He shivered. "I'm sorry, Herold," he said. "I don't know what happened. We're trying to think what to do."

The crow subsided, though the wiffling noise that came from his closed beak was almost a hiss.

They were interrupted just then by Gogs, who quite often found an excuse to come down the road about the time school was coming out. Although he had never been terribly good at things like reading and arithmetic, he missed being with his friends since he had been stopped from going to the school. He was carrying a twisted bit of rusty iron on his shoulder and holding another in his hand. His curly red hair was a shade darker than usual, as though he had been under a shower of rust. Which was pretty well where he had been. "It's off the ridge-plough," he explained with one of his broad grins. "It broke. We were putting in turnips. I've to take it to the smiddy."

His eyes grew round with amazement when he heard Sparrow's story. "What will you do?"

he asked. It was never any use asking Gogs for advice.

The others were silent.

"Why should an otter know anything about it anyway?" Kittel said.

"Otters eat fish," Bull said. "My gran says that anything that eats fish gets wise."

"Even so," said Kittel, who didn't take the sayings of Bull's grandmother all that seriously.

"You should do what it said," said Bull. "You should take the shape of your stone."

Sparrow fingered the rough pyramid-shape of the shrunken mountain in his pouch. "I have," he said. "It doesn't make any difference; it's just like being changed into any other shape."

"Wait till you can see the Pole Star," said Bull. "Then try it."

"That's a good idea," said Gogs. "You should try that." He made his piece of iron more comfortable on his shoulder and prepared to go on down into the village. "There's something going on," he said. "My aunt's got Plato Smithers to hold a big meeting in the hall. She's been round everyone telling them they have to go to it. They won't say what it's about — but she found out about Lissie's dad taking her off to what's-its-name and she just about took a purple fit. I'll let you know if I hear any more."

As the others were thinking more about Herold's wing and linden ladies just then, they

46

didn't find this piece of news as alarming as they should have done.

Kittel arranged to be back with Sparrow when the stars came out, and then went over to hear all about Lissie's adventure in Villas. However, apart from sighing rapturously every time she mentioned the boy, Ormand, Lissie was more concerned about what had been happening since her return to Copperhill. It seemed that something had snapped in her mother after the row about her father's work and then his taking Lissie with him on his travels. Worse still, Ms Redwall had lost no time in discovering the shameful secret of their trip to Villas.

"She was there," Lissie told Kittel. "I mean, waiting in the living room with my mum. They were like a couple of china cats. We were caught red-handed. Dad looked like a little boy that's been nabbed stealing apples. It was much worse for him – I didn't really care."

"What did they say?"

"They? Mum didn't say anything. It was old Redbottom that did the talking. Honestly, Kittel, she's completely taken over the house. And Mum's gone really queer. The way she looks at you ... I think she's going mad, I'm not joking."

"What did they say?" Kittel said again.

"Oh, I don't know. All this stuff about being corrupted and 'seeing things that no young person should see', and how they weren't true-blooded human beings in the other villages – you wouldn't believe it, honestly. So I said I'd kissed Ormand and he felt quite human to me. I didn't really, I just said it to shock them. Old Redbottle just about expired, I really thought she'd had it!"

"Pity she hadn't," Kittel said thoughtfully, remembering Gog's news.

"Anyway, Dad's off again tomorrow," Lissie went on. "He said I shouldn't miss school again. But I'm worried Mum'll do something drastic when he's not there to keep an eye on me."

"Like what?"

Lissie shrugged.

When Kittel got back home, Sparrow was already waiting in the bedroom, straining his eyes into the pale northern sky, which could be seen from the window. Peering out through the whiskery thatch, gradually their eyes could make out the elusive pinpricks that were the stars. Five here, seven there, and one lonely light in a great space of sky – Cassiopeia and the Great Bear, following each other ceaselessly around the Pole Star.

"All right?" said Sparrow.

"Let me light the candle first," said Kittel quickly.

"Why? You won't see the stars so easily."

"We don't need to now," said Kittel; "we

know they're there. I don't want to be left alone in the dark."

"I'll be right here!" Sparrow exclaimed – Kittel seemed to be behaving very queerly. "I'm only changing into the stone."

"You're supposed to be looking for Puckel – and I don't know what'll happen to you when you turn into the stone."

Sparrow realized she might have a point. The fact was that, with Puckel, it was difficult to know exactly where you were. The weird, wild old man, whom Sparrow had met in the mountains, was an uncertain and magical person. Sparrow and Kittel had helped him in an attempt to recapture the dragon – indeed, the last they had seen of him was locked in desperate combat with the terrible creature, spinning off up into the higher reaches of the sky. Towards the Pole Star? It was possible.

"I'll be right here," Sparrow said again, all the same. "Nothing's going to happen – it never has before."

Nevertheless he went downstairs and lit a candle at the kitchen fire. He brought it back and put it on the little table at his bedside. For a moment, a monstrous shadow of his head flickered on the sloping ceiling of the room as a draught caught the candle flame. Then the room brightened – the shadow, and Sparrow, were gone.

*　*　*

49

Kittel waited, and watched. Kittel, too, had a remarkable gift, though as far as she knew no one had given it to her — at least not in the way Sparrow had been given his gifts by Puckel. Kittel could see through shape-changes. Sparrow had never been able to hide from her by taking another thing's shape. Just now she could see him within the stone's shape, still gazing out northwards. What else *could* have happened? A puff and a bang, and Puckel appearing? It was no different from times before, it was just like changing into any other thing's shape.

"It's no use, Sparrow," she said. "Nothing's going to happen. You'd better change back."

The candle flickered a little from her breath. There was no answer from Sparrow.

"Sparrow?" said Kittel. "Can you hear me?"

Something had happened after all. Kittel waited. An hour, maybe, until her eyelids grew heavy and she found she had nodded off to sleep.

The candle guttered. She opened the drawer to take out another, but there was none there. Sparrow was always running out. It was at times like this that she longed for an electric light with a switch near to hand. By the time she had carried the candle through to her own room, it had gone out. She hesitated, then groped her way to her bed and settled herself to sleep.

50

The morning sun woke her. She leaped up and ran back through to Sparrow's room. The stone was still on the table where it had been before. Sparrow was still in its shape, gazing northwards.

Kittel turned it round. Sparrow went on staring. She didn't like to leave it there. Murie didn't know about it and might throw it out – anyway, she felt uneasily that she ought to keep an eye on it. She told Murie Sparrow had left early in the morning but that she was expecting him at school in time. That was true, in a way. She did Sparrow's jobs as well as her own, and set off for school herself.

Lissie was not at school again, although she had said she would be. Sparrow stayed in the stone's shape all day. Kittel's anxiousness grew. After school she screwed up her courage, and went and knocked at the door of Lissie's house.

Lissie's mother appeared. She looked wild and dishevelled and grey, which shocked Kittel considerably; Ms Clodish was the neatest and most house-proud person in the village. She didn't seem to look at Kittel but somewhere over her shoulder. She seized a broom that was beside the door and brandished it at Kittel's feet. "Out," she said. "All dirt goes out – out – out!" Then she slammed the door again. Kittel could only hope Lissie had gone with her father after all.

51

In the evening of the next day – the day after the meeting – Kittel slunk down to the village square and stood listening amongst the linden trees outside the hall. There were murmurings of a crowd of people inside, but she could make nothing out. The stone rams' heads glared down balefully at her from the gables.

Kittel went miserably home. She had had to tell Murie what had happened with Sparrow so that Murie wouldn't send out search parties. Now Murie was as worried and jumpy as she was. They quarrelled, and went to bed early. Kittel kept the stone by her bedside, and Sparrow went on staring.

The next morning, only about half of the school turned up. There were none of the little ones, and of the older ones only those who lived on the edge of the village – like Bull, who had come down the road with her.

"Well," Kittel said when they realized that as many children as would be coming had come, "I said I would tell you what I know about evolution, so that's what I'll do. Where I come from, everyone says that people came down from monkeys. But Sparrow says a very, very old rat once told him that people had come from rats. Anyway—"

"Where is Sparrow?" asked one of the children.

"He's – he's away just now," Kittle stammered. "For a – a little. He'll be back soon. Anyway, I was saying—"

She never got any further, because at that moment the classroom door opened and Ms Redwall swept in, followed by the huge form of Plato Smithers. Everyone stared in silence.

Ms Redwall sailed to the front of the class, but Plato Smithers hung back, looming in the doorway and looking a little embarrassed. Kittel suspected that the big man had never been in front of a class before and was feeling he ought to try and squeeze in at one of the desks.

Ms Redwall placed herself almost on top of Kittel, who stepped back. "All right, Mr Smithers," she said. "Do your duty."

Smithers shuffled forwards towards Kittel. He was holding his felt hat in his hands and wringing it repeatedly as though it were soaking wet. "Well, miss, it's like this," he said, looking at Kittel's feet. "We need you to make a promise, you see..."

The sight of the huge man being so bashful about speaking to a young girl was making the class whisper and giggle. Ms Redwall drew herself up, quelled them with a terrible stare, then turned towards Kittel. "Continue, Mr Smithers," she said coldly.

"Well," Plato Smithers went on, "if you can make this promise and keep it, well, everything will be all right. But if you can't make it, then

I'm afraid that this village just isn't the place for you. We know you've said you can't remember where you came from, but—"

"But we think that a couple of nights out alone in the mountains will soon bring your memory back," Ms Redwall put in. And she shuddered till her pink double chins were shaking too.

Kittel swallowed. "What is the promise?" she asked.

"Well," Plato Smithers said, "you must promise not to speak to any of the young ones in the village again."

"How old do they have to be before I can speak to them?" Kittel asked innocently.

Her simple question threw Plato Smithers into such confusion that he was left quite speechless. He was not a man who thought very quickly – nor was he a harsh man.

But Ms Redwall was there for that very reason. "Doesn't that just prove everything I said about her?" she hissed. "Cool as a cucumber, isn't she? Have you ever seen such ice-cold impertinence? And don't think it doesn't spread, my word, no . . ." She looked as though she thought Kittel the most hateful, dangerous thing she had ever seen.

However, here Kittel saved Plato Smithers from further awkwardness. She wanted out of the whole horrible situation. Smithers she could stand, but this Redwall woman gave her the creeps. "All right," she said hurriedly, "I promise. But I'd like to say goodbye to some of my friends if I'm not to speak to them again."

Plato Smithers didn't look at Ms Redwall — probably, Kittel thought, in case she made him say no. "That seems quite reasonable to me, miss," he said. "Just you go ahead and do that." He seemed relieved.

But now Kittel sprang her surprise. "Thank you," she said politely. "And, just so that you know I'll be keeping my promise, I'll do the other thing you want, too. I'll leave the village."

In the stunned silence that followed this announcement, Kittel, holding herself very straight, walked out of the school.

4

THE POLE TOWER

To begin with, turning into the stone was like all the other times he had tried it before. Sparrow felt his pyramid-shape, his coldness, his hardness, the slight confusion from not needing to breathe any more, the inner silence that came because there was no blood rushing round his body. There was nothing new in all that.

But he couldn't see Kittel, and he should have been able to; in fact, he couldn't see any of his bedroom. In the form of a stone he could normally see all round him at once. Now, he could see nothing – no bedroom, no Kittel, no candlelight. It panicked him, and he tried to change back to his own shape, but couldn't. Nothing happened. He was alone, in darkness. Could Kittel see him? Even if she could, how would she know he was in trouble?

Sparrow's panic didn't last. Stones aren't

made to panic. After a moment or two, he began to do what stones always do, which is wait.

At last – whether it was sooner or later he couldn't tell, because stones don't feel quick or slow either – there was light again, the tiny, distant light of a star: the Pole Star, in the midst of an empty space of sky. Rapidly it grew brighter. Soon it was as bright as a clear, freezing night of winter, and it grew brighter yet. It was twice – five times – as bright as the Pole Star ought to be. Ten times. There were no other stars to be seen, but gradually a pale mist seemed to form round this one, to become brighter, to glow like starlight. The mist took on edges. It was a spiral, a glowing, silver spiral that slowly turned about the Pole Star...

Sparrow was approaching the edge of the spiral – whether walking or floating, and whether from below or above, he could not tell. Whichever it was, he had reached the outer arm of it. It was turning in his direction; that is, he found himself moving along the spiral arm. It was like travelling along a road of glimmering mist.

On and on he went, until he realized from his circling motion that he must be near the centre of the spiral. Did that mean he was approaching the Pole? There seemed to be something ahead of him, though there was no longer any sign of the star. There was a faint blue light, but most of the thing – whatever it was – was black as midnight.

Then Sparrow realized – or had come close enough to see – that what he was approaching was a tower – a peculiarly-shaped tower, thin at top and bottom, fatter in the middle, like an elongated egg. There was a single lighted window. He must have been floating, he thought, for next moment he was at the window, peering in, with his nose pressed against a cold pane of thick, bumpy glass.

Because the glass was so bumpy, it was hard to make anything out at first. There seemed to be a small, bare room with a bed, some shelves, and a small, round table. But next moment – coming towards him with a strange, waving motion because of the uneven glass – he saw Puckel.

It was so strange, seeing the old man so unexpectedly after so long! And so frustrating, too, because although he was quite close, the glass of the window made him seem almost as distant as if Sparrow were looking at him through the wrong end of a bad telescope. Yet there was nothing strange, or distant, about the croaky old voice that snapped right in his ear. "That took you long enough," Puckel said.

The old man was unchanged. His wild white hair still looked as though several bird's nests might be concealed in it; his brown skin still looked like an old leather purse that had lain in water and then dried in the sun; and even through that glass, there was no mistaking those piercing, wild green eyes that were like living pools among the rocks. In his hand he held the curious, gnarled stick he always had – even more twisted than usual, because of the glass – and on his face Sparrow could make out the familiar scowl that he had long ago decided Puckel must put on to stop himself bursting out into uncontrollable laughter.

The only thing that was different about him was his cloak. The shabby old green and brown thing he had always worn, that smelled of must and mushrooms and sometimes looked more tatters than cloak, was gone. In its place Puckel wore a splendid, sweeping coat of dark blue with silver embroidery around the collar and cuffs, and a coiling silver brooch. He would have looked very magnificent if he had not seemed so out of place in it: its splendour just made him look more like an old tramp than ever.

Sparrow tried to ignore the old man's complaint. "I like your new coat," he said.

"Stuff and nonsense," Puckel snorted. Although Sparrow could barely see his mouth moving because of the distorting glass, the voice was as clear as if the pair of them had been sitting next to each other.

"It's very grand," Sparrow persisted.

"Absolutely unnecessary. It was part of the

agreement, and if you ask me, calculated to make a donkey out of me."

"What agreement?" Sparrow enquired.

"I came to an agreement with the dragon."

"You mean you didn't beat the dragon?"

"You don't really beat dragons," Puckel said carelessly; "at best, you try to knock 'em about a bit so that you can make an arrangement with them. That's what I've done. It's a nuisance, and it keeps me tied up here, but at least it keeps him out of mischief. Someone would need to call his name out before he could get back to earth — but no one knows his name, so it doesn't matter."

As Puckel said this, Sparrow thought he turned a strangely searching glance on him — though it was difficult to tell through that thick glass. "Where is the dragon?" he asked, glancing anxiously over his shoulder.

"You came in along his tail," Puckel said.

"I came here along a sort of road of mist," Sparrow said.

"You came along his tail," Puckel repeated firmly. "Young man, it's time you learned a bit more about what's what. What took you so long, anyway?"

"Well, I didn't know how to find you!" Sparrow exclaimed indignantly. "I didn't even know if you wanted me to find you."

"What do you think I left that lump of rock behind for, then?" Puckel demanded.

"I found it by accident!" Sparrow protested. "I thought you'd forgotten it."

"Hmph!" Puckel snorted.

"What's happening?" Sparrow exclaimed, for the glass seemed to have begun to move, like thick water, and Puckel and the room began to waver and pull out of shape.

"It's because we were talking about you-know-who," came Puckel's voice, as the room seemed to make an effort to straighten itself out again. "It's difficult enough to get him to sleep up here in the ordinary course of things – so as soon as we start talking about him he moves in his sleep. Better tell me what you have to tell me before we get dragged out of shape altogether – or he wakes up."

Sparrow told Puckel about his meeting with the linden lady and the otter. As he spoke, Puckel and the room in the tower became reasonably clear again, though every so often a corner of what he could see would start drifting off into a swirl of colour.

"Hm," Puckel grunted when he had finished. "You brought all that on yourself, so don't ask me for sympathy."

"How?" Sparrow gasped.

"By trying to get to Kittel's place out of time, of course. There's a time for you to get to Kittel's place and a time to stay put. It was a false move. You've a lot of things to learn before you can make that journey."

"But I thought—" Sparrow began.

"What you thought," Puckel interrupted, "was based on some nonsense that crazy old schoolteacher told you about a wall of dragon's breath that no one could get past. Well, I've news for you: it's a lot more complicated than that, and as I say, you've a lot of things to learn first — like the Secret Way of the Mountains, and the secret of the Hollywell . . ."

"The Secret Way of the Mountains," Sparrow murmured after him, remembering that these were the very words the otter had used.

". . . these things are needed," Puckel was saying, because the Polymorphs have to be controlled. All that about a stone being moved from where it should be to where it shouldn't be just means the Polymorphs have upset the balance between the Star Wheel and the Vault of the Bear. That throws the whole balance out and it'll lead to disaster if it's not checked soon."

"And what—" Sparrow began again.

"The Polymorphs, boy," Puckel interrupted in a low, solemn voice, "are masters of the dragon's dreaming."

Sparrow felt his own voice sinking to a whisper. "And what's that?" he asked. He had always found talk of the dragon's dreams unsettling.

"Mind-stuff, that's what — all that comes into your mind; the rock that feels hard to your hand and the hand that feels the rock.

The wind that blows from the way you're facing to the emptiness that's behind you. It's all there because that's how you think it. All things are made of thought. These masters of the dreaming are quicker than thought; they break up the way you expect the world to be and puff! the world vanishes like smoke, and you're left with chaos – madness."

Sparrow had an inspiration. "Like the skewered meat and Herold's wing!" he said.

"Exactly like that," Puckel nodded sagely. "Things would all swim together if the balance moved too much in the Polymorphs' favour. The dish would run away with the spoon. It's no laughing matter. Up to now we have kept the Polymorphs in check – I, and those who work with me. Now we can't any more, because I'm stuck up here with my pet lizard."

"So how can you set the balance right, now?" Sparrow asked.

"I need you to control them," Puckel said.

Sparrow thought back to his encounter with the linden lady. Yes, he thought – perhaps, with the shrunken mountain, he could learn to control them . . .

"You needn't start thinking along those lines," Puckel said sharply, as though he guessed Sparrow's thoughts. "They're a lot trickier than you think. They take many forms; they can be in many places at once; they are not easy to master. You had a very close shave

63

with the creature you met. The food it offered you was the shape you were in – the crow's shape. If you had eaten it, you would have been eating your own chosen shape. You would have vanished. You would have been in limbo. It could have happened."

Sparrow listened in horror. "Is that what she was trying to do to me?" he asked.

"I suppose you thought you were living in some sort of mountain wonderland where nothing bad ever happened," said Puckel. He sighed, and then spoke more gently. "Well, it might have been – once. It should have been. But things haven't been as they were meant to be in these mountains, not for many a long year now.

"It all comes back to the dragon being out of his proper place, of course. There hasn't been much we could do about that, but we've got by, in most respects. Nothing's been what you'd call satisfactory – one result which you would notice is the way the people of the different villages have fallen out of touch with each other. The Polymorphs have cast their shadow over all the lands between them. Now each village is like an island in a sea of shadow."

"But I've been going miles from the village for ages," Sparrow objected, "and nothing's ever happened to me before."

"That stone's played its part in protecting you up to now," said Puckel. "But they've just been biding their time, ever since I left the mountains. They had no reason to hurry. Now they've moved at last, and as soon as you made a false move, they were in there – like mould into a broken fruit.

"They have certain ways of trapping you. Eni and Tho get in there, under the skin, if you fall into a quarrel; Ur offers you food to eat, or hides common things in a cloak of deceit and seeming; Eych plays on your fears, and can strike you dumb or blind; Yo lies in wait if you get a swollen idea of yourself. They don't always work the same way, but these are the most common. I expect it was Ur you met. Bur it certainly wasn't: that's their leader. If you'd met Bur you'd have known about it ! The six Polymorphs, with Bur their leader." He fell silent.

"What am I supposed to do then?" said Sparrow. He had started to feel very small, lost amid a world of unguessed dangers.

"Now you're talking sense," Puckel answered. "'Supposed to do' is the kind of talk I like to hear. There are two things which can be done. One – the better – would be to loose the dragon on the creatures; that would bring them to heel immediately. But of course, that's not possible . . ."

As he said this, Sparrow thought the old man glanced at him again, with a strange gleam in his green eyes. But he scarcely paused in what he was saying. "The other," he went on, "is to learn the Secret Way of the Mountains and continue to do what I was doing until I was forced to come up here—"

"What? Me alone?" Sparrow burst out.

"Why not?" Puckel replied. "You're good enough material. Some bits missing, of course – one big one in particular. That'll need patching up to begin with."

"What part of me's missing?"

"The part you've never known, and so never missed."

Sparrow looked anxiously down at himself.

"I don't mean a bit's fallen off you, numb-skull – now look what we've done..." Puckels' voice suddenly grew dimmer, and the swimming and swirling of the glass got rapidly worse.

Sparrow thought he heard Puckel saying something about his mother, but he couldn't make out what, because the old man's voice had become fuzzy and indistinct. Sparrow felt he was slipping altogether out of reach. "What bit?" he cried, as a feeling like panic began to grow in the pit of his stomach. "What bit's missing?" But there was no answer, and the swimming and swirling of shapes was going on all round him. He guessed it was the dragon moving again, and waited for things to clear. But minutes passed and there was no sign of anything he could recognize: even the swirling colours were fading, as though he were plunging gradually into deep water.

"Return as soon as maybe!" Puckel's voice seemed to call, out of a great distance, and then everything became very confused. He had a glimpse of the village hall in Copperhill, but all from the wrong angle, and Ms Redwall striding across the picture from top corner to bottom corner waving her arms about. He saw one of the stone rams' heads on the hall gable looking round and winking at him. Then there was blue sky and clouds, and the waving of Ms Redwall's arms became the flapping of a dark wing which blotted out the light.

"Look at that! Just look at that!" Herold's voice came screeching. "There's a part of me missing – there's a big part of me missing! And Sparrow saw once again the half-moon of chewed-off feathers, only where there should have been empty space there was something like an egg stuck to the edge of the wing. "My feather!" Herold's voice screeched again. "See it? It's missing! My father, that's what that is. My father – faa – faa!"

Then complete darkness, complete silence, fell, and Sparrow found himself sobbing, and whispering through the sobs: "My father, that's what's missing. My father – my father . . ." until all at once the breath left him and he was utterly still, waiting.

5

THE SHADOW

It was two days from the closing of the school before Kittel saw Lissie again – two awful, anxious days in which she stopped even peering at the stone to see if there was any change in Sparrow. Lissie suddenly appeared at the door. Her normally rosy cheeks were pale and she looked gaunt and hollow-eyed.

"Where have you been?" Kittel gasped. "What's wrong? Where's your dad?"

"He's up at Bull's gran's," Lissie said. "Oh, Kittel, it's been awful!"

"Where were you? What happened? I thought you must be away!"

"I was in the wash-house."

"What? Why? You mean – locked in?"

Lissie nodded. "As soon as my dad went away. She took a hold of me and told me my clothes were filthy and I was to get in to the wash-house and take them off. I said, they're fine Mum, or something like that, and she went on repeating 'fine Mum, fine Mum', to everything I said. It was horrible. Then she pushed me into the wash-house and locked the door before I realized what she was doing. Then she said I was a cat and cats belong in cages."

"Did you get food?"

"She pushed it under the door."

"What about – "

"I used the boiler as a toilet, if that's what you mean. She can boil her clothes in it if she likes. I never want to go back there again – never." Lissie's voice shook, but her face remained hard. "Dad came back and let me out just now. I thought he was going to kill her. I've heard about the meeting – and the school."

"This wouldn't have happened to you if it hadn't been for the Redwall," Kittel said in a low voice.

"I don't know," Lissie said. "Mum didn't have to be like that. She didn't have to do everything Redwall said, did she?"

"Yes," Murie said when they went indoors, "a visit to Mrs Hind sounds like an excellent idea. Let's go over there right now and have a conference."

A voice spoke again at Sparrow's ear, but it

was not Puckel's. This was a voice Sparrow seemed to know quite well, though he couldn't think who it belonged to. A woman's voice, perhaps...

"Once the Traders' work was honoured as it should be," the voice said. "People in Copperhill knew there wouldn't be much hay or harvest taken in if it wasn't for the fine scythe blades from Drakewater. In Springing Wood people knew they wouldn't be able to brew their fine apple spirit without the copper coils from our village. And so it went round.

"I don't know what happened. Something must have gone bad. The Traders call it the Shadow. They say the villages are like little islands in a great sea of shadow. The forests and the rivers and the mountainsides look good – but there's an unseen danger in them always there, always waiting.

"Few people know of the risks the Traders run. Once they did. When my son was killed – when his horse went wild and threw him, then turned on him and trampled him – people just said, 'Well, what do you expect with a Trader?' You can't blame them, really. Those dangers are always there. It's been known for men to go crazy and throw themselves shrieking over a cliff. I don't say that's what happened to Mistress Overton's father or her husband, for they weren't Traders, and no one knows..."

Because it was all so quiet inside him,

Sparrow could hear everything very clearly. He had a feeling that the voice was not speaking to him; there were other people there somewhere listening to it. But where was he? And why couldn't he see anything?

"But the Traders believe they're protected," the voice was saying. "The tale's still told among them of how once – a bad time it must have been, for there were eight of them all together, for safety, up on the Old Road – all of a sudden they heard music and singing in the trees. Before they knew what was happening, they were dancing to the music and, believe it or not, their horses started dancing too. But this was no ordinary dancing. No, they were dancing up and down like dolls on a string, and they couldn't stop. They danced from noon of one day right through the night and into the afternoon of the next day.

"It seemed they must dance themselves to death – but just in time they were rescued. A man appeared, dressed all over in bright, shining copper, with a bear's head for a hood. He slashed his long, bright knife at the trees where the music was coming from, and the sound died away to a whimpering and the men and horses were able to stop their dancing. The man with the bear hood said he was the Guardian and that he was there to protect the Traders from the Danger of the Road.

"He has been seen again since then, not once

but many times. We say that as long as the Traders use the road, the Guardian will be there to protect them; and as long as the Guardian's there to protect the Traders, the villages will be safe. But down in the villages no one speaks of these things any more – they pretend the other villages don't exist, they pretend they don't know what the Traders do.

"But what if, sometimes, the Guardian goes away? He wasn't there to protect my son. I remember it was in that same year – the very same year that Mistress Overton's husband went missing – the apple blossom fell early from the trees and there were no apples that autumn. I say the Shadow came into the village that year, even though it went away again. Perhaps that's what's happening now with that donkey-of-a-neighbour of yours, Don."

Then a man's voice said, "Yet there's been no sign of anything wrong up on the Road – else I'd never have taken Lissie."

Then Sparrow realized who the speaker was. The man who was killed by the horse was Bull's father, which meant that it was Bull's grandmother speaking – and obviously she was speaking to Don Clodish. But how was he hearing her?

With an effort, he realized that he was again in the shape of the stone – if he had ever been out of it. "Polymorphs!" he exclaimed, and changed back into himself.

"Sparrow! Where did you come from? Where have you been?" seemed to burst from half a dozen people all round him. He seemed to be sitting, gazing into a small, bright fire. Then –

"Ow! Get off!" a voice bellowed in his ear, and a hefty shove landed him crack on a wooden floor. He looked up, bewildered, and realized straight away that he must have been sitting on Kittel's knee when he took his own shape again. They weren't alone, and they weren't in Sparrow's bedroom. They were in the kitchen of Bull's house, and apart from Kittel, there was Mrs Hind herself, Bull, Don Clodish, Murie and Lissie.

"How did I get here?" Sparrow said, rubbing the leg he had fallen on.

"I brought you," Kittel said, "in my pocket." She seemed unaccountably angry. "And don't you ever do a thing like that to me again!"

"Or me," Murie put in, from the other side of the room.

"What do you mean?" Sparrow said. "What have I done?"

"What have you done?" Kittel railed. "Oh, only been away for five days and nights. Only left us thinking you'd be nothing but a lump of rock for the rest of your life."

"I was just away for a few minutes," Sparrow protested, uncomfortably aware that Mrs Hind and Don Clodish, who knew nothing about

Sparrow's shape-changing, were looking rather confused.

"I can assure you Kittel is quite right," Murie said; "and I'm beginning to think your tricks are getting just a bit dangerous and out of hand."

Kittel realized that Sparrow was anxious not to discuss his magical doings in front of everyone; and despite her anger, she changed the subject, though with a look that plainly warned: "you've not heard the last from me!" What she said out loud was, "Anyway, you couldn't have chosen a better time to be away."

"Why?" said Sparrow. "What's happened?"

"Oh, nothing much," said Kittel, "except that the school's been closed, and I've been told to get out of the village."

"*What!?*" exclaimed Sparrow, unable to believe his ears. "But – how – how – what – they can't..."

"We'll have to go to the cottage," said Sparrow after everything had been explained to him. "We'll get Kittel home to her place, then I'll come back here. If they don't want a teacher, they don't have to have one." Sparrow had already forgotten Puckel's warning about the time having to be right.

"And how long will it take you to find how to get to Kittel's place?" said Murie.

Sparrow shrugged.

"What about the winter?" Bull said, taking

74

up Murie's question. "It's all right going for a picnic in the mountains, but what if you have to spend a long time searching for a way? Supposing you're still searching in October? How will you manage then, when the bad weather starts and Kittel's not allowed to come back to the village? You'd die out there in the mountains."

"I could come with you," Don Clodish said unexpectedly. "Lissie would come too. We'd been going to leave here and go to Villas, but it's all one really. If we did that, we could help prepare the house for the winter, and Kittel could come back to it if she couldn't find her way home."

"I'll come as well," said Bull; "I want to help too."

"You need to stay and look after your gran," Don Clodish said.

After much argument, both on that day and the next, it was agreed that Murie and Gogs should be the ones who would go with Sparrow and Kittel to the Valley of Murmuring Water. Murie, who was feeling a little impatient with the talk of invisible shadows and guardians who couldn't be relied on to do much guarding, simply felt so angry with the people of Copperhill that she wanted to leave the village and would have been quite happy never to come back. Gogs particularly wanted to come because his family was divided over the whole business of Kittel. His mother was standing by her sister, and had never cared much for Kittel anyway. His father, like many others, was deeply shocked at the decision to put Kittel out of the village. He secretly encouraged Gogs to go with Sparrow's party because he believed it would do a lot of damage to Ms Redwall's cause if her own nephew left the village in support of Kittel.

Murie was leaving the house for Bull to look after. Bull was none too happy at being left behind, but he saw that he couldn't leave his grandmother without help. Murie's hens were to be left behind, but the cow and the goats were to go with them, and they were also to take two large bags of meal, gardening tools and vegetables to plant. It was all a bit hare-brained, but Murie thought that if they worked hard to begin with, they might just manage. "If we run out, Sparrow will just have to fly back and steal some more," she said.

Don Clodish decided that things would not remain safe for himself or Lissie with Ms Redwall right next door, so he decided to go on with his plan to leave Copperhill with Lissie and settle in Villas.

There was a painful parting between Kittel and Lissie. The two friends realized they might never see each other again, however things turned out. Both girls felt, in their different ways, that they were being forced to leave the village. Lissie didn't think her father would ever come back to live at Copperhill.

"He's going to rebuild the ruined house in Ormand's garden," she said. "He says he'll have to come back for Mum when it's ready, because he doesn't think she'll be able to look after herself, the way she's going. Perhaps he's right, I don't know. I hate her – I really do – but I suppose we can't just abandon her."

Kittel said nothing, and Lissie fell silent too. Now that the thing had actually happened, neither of them wanted to say the word "mad".

As Lissie watched her friend walking off under the elms by the street out of the village, she felt that the whole world she had known was coming to an end. "Well, that just leaves Ormand," she told herself; and the thought of his surprised-looking eyes, under his cap of fuzzy brown hair, comforted her.

On the morning of the fourth day after Ms Redwall's meeting, Sparrow, Kittel, Murie and Gogs, along with the cow and the goat and its kid, set off on their journey into the mountains. They each had a heavy pack to carry, while the cow was laden as well, and the goat, much to its disgust, was harnessed to the small goat sledge.

It was a grey, drizzly morning, and none of them felt in the least adventurous – apart from the kid, which did mountaineering exploits on its mother's back. They looked back at the low, white house with its rain-darkened thatch and dripping eaves, and the cloak of grey cloud behind it, and seemed to feel the same grey coldness inside them. The house meant everything that was safe and warm and secure, that they were leaving behind.

From his flights in crow-form, Sparrow now knew the way well, and their journey through the forest, if slow and soaking, was uneventful – apart from troubles with the goat. Occasionally Sparrow had to unhitch it from the sledge so that he could fly, with the various sacks and bundles, over some particularly rough part of the ground. He could do this quite easily, as he never felt the weight of anything he carried when he was flying, but after he had finished there would be a mad chase as they tried to recapture the sulky creature. A couple of times Sparrow had to take its shape in order to bring it back to the harness, and then had to endure the goat hissing reproaches at him under its breath for the next half-hour.

Not long after lunchtime on the second day, the grey clouds broke up, and pale blue sky, then sparkling sunlight, followed. It was at that stage that Herold caught up with them. Sparrow had been feeling very pleased with himself for having given the crow the slip, because Herold was bound to object to him and Kittel flying off to search out her way home.

He realized he should have known better. "Now I'm for it," he muttered as the crow descended on them with a triumphant squawk.

Herold perched on the branch of a tree and gave Sparrow a long harangue on the virtues of loyalty and steadfastness. Although the others couldn't understand his speech, it was obvious that Sparrow was getting a good scolding. When they laughed, Herold got so infuriated that he lost his balance and finished up on the next branch down. There, he took a deep breath, stuck his beak in the air and, taking on an expression of great dignity, told Sparrow he had decided to return to the home of his fathers and that it was a mere accident that they were going the same way.

Sparrow took a biscuit from his pouch and crumbled it. "Would you like something to eat?" he said.

Herold accepted this offer promptly, but refused to eat from Sparrow's hand like – he said – a pet parrot. He stood by his word, too, and didn't journey with them. Sparrow wondered if this new mood would last long enough for him to be able to get away with Kittel, when the time came.

Near the end of the fourth day from leaving Copperhill they arrived at Sparrow's cottage.

No one found the valley very welcoming, even after three nights in the open. The cottage looked like a gigantic bee-skep in the twilight, rearing up in the gloom of an alien place. Even the fragrance of lush grass and meadowsweet and sun-warmed pine that filled the air seemed unfamiliar and threatening.

Sparrow creaked open the massive, five-cornered door. It was pitch dark inside, but he easily found his way to the corner where the bedding material was piled. It had to be spread out rather, as there were four of them and not two as he had originally expected; but they had brought blankets, and no one could deny that it was the cosiest night they had spent since leaving Copperhill.

Plato Smithers was now finding little time for his work as a stonemason. He seemed to spend all his days cramped in the little room at the back of the village hall where he had his office. The room was barely big enough for him to sit at the broad oak desk with his legs stretched out, and the only times he really liked it were when he had a bottle of parsnip wine to keep him company. But there wasn't much chance of that these days, as the reason why he was being kept busy in his office was that Ms Redwall kept pestering him. Ms Redwall didn't approve of his drinking parsnip wine.

On this particular morning, just over a week after her famous meeting, she had been in to tell him that as the children of the village were now desperately in need of proper schooling, she was prepared, "for the good of the community", to take over the school where Ms Minn had left off a year and a half ago. Smithers said he would "think about it".

Plato Smithers had found Kittel a puzzle ever since she had arrived in the village. He was inclined to think that she really came from one of the other villages, whatever she might say, and that her stories of a world of incredible machines and huge cities were mere make-believe. On the other hand, there was the question of her amazing knowledge. There was no doubt she had taught the youngsters how to read. He had even learned a word himself. Up on a dusty shelf in a corner of the office there was a television. Beside one of the buttons were some of the white squiggles which Kittel said were letters. They made the word "POWER".

Plato Smithers sighed several times and shook his head several times. This meant he was thinking.

The door opened and Bull Hind came in.

"Well, lad?" Smithers said. Ms Redwall had particularly complained about Bull on several occasions.

"There's something you should know," said Bull. "Kittel's gone, but she hasn't gone alone."

Plato Smithers shifted uncomfortably. He had, of course, heard that Sparrow's house at Overton was empty. "Well?" he said, trying to look as though it had nothing to do with him.

"There's four of them went," Bull said; and smiled grimly as he saw Smithers' fingers moving slightly on the table: the big man was trying to count out if he had the names of four missing people.

Eventually he sat up, scratched his head, and looked hard at Bull. "Who else?"

"Gogs Westward."

You could almost hear the sound of Smithers' brain working. Then he blurted out, "But that's – her nephew!"

"That's right," said Bull, and left the room.

Smithers leaped to his feet and roared after Bull as he made his way up the side of the hall, "Where have they gone?"

Bull turned, fixed Plato Smithers with his coldest stare, and shrugged. "How should I know?" he said.

As Plato Smithers settled himself in bed that night, his none-too-quick brain was in a spin. That afternoon he had learned – through yet another of Ms Redwall's visits – that Don Clodish had left Copperhill and had taken Lissie with him again. "The whole fabric of society is collapsing!" Ms Redwall had wailed.

Smithers did not sleep that night. Never had such things happened before in his life. People didn't leave the village – especially young girls. The deep fear which the people of the village had, but never spoke about, never thought about – the fear whose cause was only remembered by the Traders – came over him. "It wasn't right," he muttered to himself. "It wasn't right. It should never have been done . . ."

In the forests somewhere between the village and the Valley of Murmuring Water, a strange music was playing softly in the branches of the trees, drifting slowly westwards. Only the night creatures heard it, a meandering, unreal sort of music, sometimes like the thin, reedy music of pipes, sometimes mixed with a deeper thrumming and twanging like drawn strings. Owls shifted restlessly, the snouts of hedgehog and badger worked this way and that, as if trying to pick up an elusive scent. But there was no scent – only a pale shadow that crept about the foot of the trees or high in the topmost branches, following wherever the music led. A shadow that wavered and broke like mist, but was not mist.

Softly westwards the music and the pale shadow crept, and down through the woods of birch and rowan above the village of Copperhill, while another arm of it ran like a gentle tide along the Old Road – where Lissie and Don Clodish had gone only the day before – flowing gently at last into the great oak forests of Villas.

As the dawn came, the pale shadow faded, leaving something that the wild creatures could only sense, as animals can sense a thunderstorm or an earthquake – a feeling that something had changed, something had grown less certain, less reliable, more dangerous. Only Puckel, wandering as he once did in the forests, would have known it was a sign that the Polymorphs' power was now growing fast – though if Puckel had been there in the forests, and not trapped up among the stars, the Polymorphs would never have dared to move beyond their limits.

6

A TEST RUN

"Come on, we've got months of work to do all in a few days!"

That was the brisk message Murie woke them up with on their first morning at the cottage. She seemed to have left her normal, easy-going self at Copperhill, as they found out when she started giving them a seemingly endless list of jobs to do.

She soon had Sparrow and Gogs sweating and groaning, digging over the ground at top speed to get the vegetable seedlings planted. "We won't get much of a crop," she said, "but every little helps."

They took it in turns to stop the goats and the cow from trampling the area of grass which Murie decided would be for cutting hay – they had to have hay at all costs to keep the animals through the winter.

That was the only rest any of them got, and the goats made sure it was never too restful.

In all, the four of them were working flat out for a fortnight, day after day in the growing heat of the summer. Herold came and went, but was never there long enough for Sparrow to know if he was still in disgrace or not. The crow certainly never came for food. It was a fortnight in which there was no time for anything but work, eating (never enough of that) and sleep (even less of that). There was no time for thinking. Sparrow almost forgot about Puckel and the Polymorphs and finding Kittel's home: they seemed like vague, uneasy dreams out on the edge of a world of sweat and hot sunshine and his aching back.

At the end of the fortnight, Murie said the work could now go on at a more relaxed pace. But she added that Sparrow and Kittel should set out the very next day on the next stage of their journey. Straight away, all the uncertainties and worries about the way ahead came back to Sparrow in a rush. They might be safe enough here in the Valley of Murmuring Water, but just beyond was the gully where he and Herold had been ensnared.

Sparrow had never gone against Puckel's instructions before, and the truth was he didn't really mean to now. It was just such a long time since he had spoken with Puckel. And at that time Puckel hadn't known that Kittel was going to be put out of the village – at least, Sparrow told himself that he hadn't.

He didn't tell Kittel about his worries. He did mumble that he ought to go and see Puckel, but she refused to let him. "You're not going off to see him just now, and that's all there is to it," she said. "Last time you changed into that stone we didn't see you for nearly a week. I'm not hanging about here that long every time you can't make up your own mind about something."

Kittel had had to screw herself up to go; now she was afraid that any delay might make her change her mind. Besides, as Gogs pointed out, the quicker Kittel went, the sooner their problems would be over.

"I wish I could come too," Gogs said, "but I think I'll be needed here." Murie nodded grimly.

The following morning Murie and Gogs were out to see Sparrow and Kittel off. Murie wrapped up enough food – mostly hard little bread-biscuits and cheese to last them a good few days – and Kittel slung the package on to her front.

"Make sure you turn back when you've eaten *half* your food," Murie warned, "not the whole lot." They expected to be back again in a few days to let Murie and Gogs know how things looked. The only other thing they took with them was Sparrow's stone.

"Good luck," Gogs said; and "Be as quick as you can," said Murie. Herold was, thankfully, nowhere to be seen. Sparrow lifted Kittel off the ground and rose up with her into the clear, mid-summer sky. Murie and Gogs watched them speed off eastwards towards the sun, rising high over the rocky ridge at the end of the valley.

"Time to start cutting hay, I think," Murie remarked to Gogs.

Sparrow was anxious to get as high as possible above the stony gully, but he need not have worried. No evil spell wrapped them round, and soon the long lake was glinting like a fat blue serpent below them.

"Whee-ee!" Sparrow called out, as a cool wind tugged at their hair and beat against their eyes. It was ages since he had last made a proper flight, and the joy and excitement of the high spaces was all coming back to him.

"Don't get too excited!" Kittel shouted over the rumbling of the air in her ears. "I don't want to join in any aerobatics!"

Beneath them the long lake came to an end in a wide waterfall that gathered itself into a stony, fast-flowing river, stretching off eastwards.

"I suppose we just keep following it!" Sparrow yelled.

"It's bound to get us out of the mountains

eventually," Kittel yelled back.

But it came as a great surprise to them both how quickly the mountains ended. It was well before lunch time when they saw one last, massive rock wall rearing up ahead of them. It was right in the path of the eastward-flowing river; but the river, which was by now broad, deep and powerful, had carved itself a deep, steep channel through it. And where it poured out at the far end (with a thundering that shook the air even where Sparrow and Kittel flew), suddenly, abruptly, the mountains stopped. Below them stretched a green land such as Sparrow had never seen before.

He circled and came down to stand on the rocky top of the ridge through which the river roared. The thunder of it made them feel the ground was dancing. The most tremendous waterfall they had ever seen crashed in gigantic steps down a cliff towards the green country far below, but they could not see the bottom because of the clouds of mist and spume thrown up by the water.

What made the green land so unutterably strange to Sparrow was that there were no mountains: it was quite flat, and stretched in paler or darker greens, until it became swallowed up in a blue haze at the edge of sight. It was all too far below to make out anything properly, apart from a line of tall grey shapes that disappeared off into the misty distances.

"What are those giant things?" Sparrow whispered.

"Electricity pylons, stupid," Kittel giggled.

Their eyes returned to the tumbled drop of rock and scree below their feet.

"Look down there!" Sparrow suddenly exclaimed. He pointed. "There's something moving."

Kittel followed his finger, and in a moment picked out something bright coloured about half-way down the long grey screes beneath them. "It's people," she said at length. "They're climbing up. I knew they'd come eventually!"

For a while they watched as two bright blobs, one red, one yellow, crawled upwards across the cliff face.

"It'd be easier if we flew down," Kittel said at last.

"All right," said Sparrow. Yet he was feeling strangely shy as he took hold of her and flew from their high perch to circle down. They found then that the climbers were actually following a narrow path which threaded its way across the cliff face, and they landed on this some distance from the strangers.

The cliff towered above them on one side and dropped away giddily on the other. They were out of sight of the great waterfall here, and though the air still throbbed with its steady boom, the noise was no longer so violent.

They waited. "Some reception committee,

two climbers," Kittel muttered.

"What did you expect?" said Sparrow absently.

She grunted. "Twenty at least, and carrying a banner with WELCOME HOME, KITTEL on it. I don't know," she finished crossly, "it's as if no one's cared, and we were so near all the time . . ."

There were actually three climbers: one was a dog, a tall, reddish, lanky animal that was now racing up towards them.

"It's a red setter!" Kittel exclaimed as it bounded closer. "Just like the one we had – Max. In fact . . ."

At that moment the dog reached them and stopped suddenly. It held its long nose out as far as it possibly could without actually moving forward, while the velvety-chocolaty end of it twitched suspiciously.

"It *is* Max," said Kittel in a soft, unbelieving, husky voice.

"How do you know?" Sparrow said.

"Because he's my dog, idiot," Kittel answered, dropping down on her knees and holding out her hand. "Max?" she said softly. "Maxy? It's me. Don't you know me?"

And then she drew back her hand rapidly, because the dog let out a long, low growl. "Max," Kittel said in a hurt voice, and then suddenly looked up towards the two advancing figures. They were in single file, and she looked at the leader without recognition. "Perhaps I was wrong," she muttered, standing up again.

But Sparrow, watching it all, knew she was not wrong. The dog did recognize her. He knew that because when it growled, Sparrow had heard it say, "Of course I know you, silly bitch; I want to know what you're doing here."

He had no time to wonder if this was just ordinary doggish behaviour, or if there was more to it, because the moment Kittel stood up again she was hailed. The figure walking behind – the one in yellow – who they now saw was smaller than the leading figure, suddenly pointed and waved and called out, "It is! It's her!" in a high, excited voice.

It was a woman and a girl who were approaching. Sparrow thought their jackets must be bright enough to glow in the dark. He felt very shabby in his old, worn clothes. When he got a proper look at the girl he got a shock: she was so like Kittel he could almost have mistaken the two of them. Then he saw that the stranger was quite a lot younger, her hair a lot darker and her skin a lot paler, and –

"It's Trina!" Kittel's voice broke in on him. "It's Trina! Trina, what are you – ? Have you – ?"

"Looking for you, of course!" the other girl burst out, running forwards past the woman. Unceremoniously she shoved the dog out of the way, grabbed Kittel by the wrist, and beamed with unbelieving happiness. "And I've found you!" she exclaimed.

At this, Max seemed to become a different dog. He started bounding about, letting out small, squeaking barks, flapping his long ears and weaving in and out between the feet of the humans, while Sparrow even heard him singing a clownish song in his tuneless dog-voice.

Above the doggish din, Sparrow heard Trina introducing the woman as her schoolteacher, Miss Meggan; while Kittel said who Sparrow was and rattled off everything that had happened to her since the plane-crash when – from Trina's point of view – she had gone missing. She did that too quickly even for Sparrow to follow, but Trina seemed to be quite satisfied with her account, while old Miss Meggan beamed and nodded and tried to pat Max's head whenever he brushed past her. After three minutes of hard talking, the two sisters were agreeing to sit down and have lunch, and a large flat rock in a wide part of the path just there seemed the ideal place.

But as they were making their way towards it, Max pushed past Sparrow and paused for a second. And Sparrow heard him growl, "Not a bite – do you hear? Not a bite of her food!"

Sparrow frowned in puzzlement. Was the dog being unfriendly? Or . . . ? No, he thought, surely not . . . Kittel would know her own sister.

The sun, moving round from noon, had almost disappeared behind the towering wall of rock, and their picnic spot was one of the few places where it still shone. The ground went on shaking, and it almost felt as if the warm slab they sat down on were trying to tremble its way to the edge of the drop. Kittel opened their satchel of provisions. "We don't have to be so careful now," she said. "We've no more searching to do."

"We're on holiday — well, sort of," Trina explained. Dad's got some special work here, just for nine months, and so we all came, and I'm doing a year at the school and, anyway, when I saw the mountains I knew I had to come and look for you but they thought I should go with someone who knew the paths properly, so Miss Meggan said she'd come. We've left the car down at the bottom there. Mum thinks I'm just being stupid, expecting to find you in these mountains, but I knew I was right, I just knew it — and I was."

"And we came to meet you just on the very same day that you came to look for us!" Kittel put in excitedly.

"This was just a sort of test expedition, to see how we got on," said Trina.

"So was ours," said Kittel, "just a test run."

"We thought we might all come with the tent when the real holidays started," said Trina.

Kittel and Trina beamed at each other. Miss

Meggan beamed benignly. Sparrow looked out over the huge expanse of flat green land, misty blue in the distance, broken here and there by the darker green of woods and the dark firm lines of roads and hedges. He could make out very little. In fact, it all seemed very vague, very misty. Was that just the haze of summer heat? Surely that misty blue reminded him of something?

"Taste this," said Kittel, handing Trina a piece of the cheese Murie had given them. "It's the best you've ever had."

"Mmm," Trina agreed, nibbling at a white crumb. "Is that what you've been living on all this time?"

"You look very well on it," said Miss Meggan kindly.

Max, lying over in the shadow of the rock, growled softly.

"I've only got peanut butter sandwiches," said Trina.

"Mmm, peanut butter sandwiches!" Kittel exclaimed in delight. "Oh, can I have one – please?"

"All right," said Trina, with a strange smile.

"You must try a peanut butter sandwich," Kittel said to Sparrow. "I used to stuff myself with them."

Sparrow was not sure he liked the sound of this, and when Max growled again he liked it even less.

Trina took a flat white thing (which Sparrow didn't recognize as bread) out of the blue bag she had been carrying, and handed it to Kittel. The sun was just catching the side of the dog's head, which was resting on the edge of the rock, and it gave him a most peculiar look.

Sparrow felt more and more strongly that there was something he ought to do. The dog was staring straight at him. Trina handed him another of the white things. Sparrow felt its soft sponginess between his fingers, and then Max growled again. "Not a bite, not a bite," Sparrow heard. Kittel sank her teeth into her own sandwich. "Go on, Sparrow," she urged, "it's really good."

Max sat up. A last ray of the sun made a slash of yellow from the top of his ear to the bottom of his jaw. Sparrow stared.

"Lie down, Max," Trina's voice came dimly, "you're putting him off. He always begs, he's awful."

Sparrow's left hand slipped into his pouch and drew out the little rough stone.

The effect was immediate, devastating, unbelievable. It started with Max, who threw back his head and let out a long, rising, wolf-like howl that seemed to echo off into some immeasurable distance. The next thing was that Trina suddenly leaped to her feet, as a tremor of the ground made their rock jump in its bed as if it had been no more than a pebble. It sounded as though half a mountain had just crashed down the waterfall.

"Trina!" Kittel yelled, sending a spray of half-chewed peanut butter sandwich spluttering out of her mouth, as she clapped her hands over her ears – and then again, in a quite different tone, *"Trina!"* for Trina had begun to change.

By now Sparrow recognized what was happening. Just as once before, there was the feeling of being flung violently backwards, falling through sickening space, yet nothing moved; and something was happening to Kittel's sister – Sparrow didn't notice the teacher – a change in her hair, in her face, something changing about her arms. The hair had disappeared from the front part of her head, her arms growing longer, the hands disappearing from the wrist... He couldn't make it out. "Trina!" Kittel screamed again. "Oh, Trina! No!"

Sparrow leaped up and grabbed hold of Kittel's arm. All about them was screaming, crashing, roaring, wailing and howling, and a distant sound that might have been the waterfall or a mighty wind getting up. It became hard to see, because the very mountainside seemed to be collapsing round them. Rocks fell, waterspouts spouted; fire seemed to be spreading over the distant green land. Dust and smoke and mist gathered. Vaguely Sparrow made out the humped shape of the Polymorph where Kittel's sister had been. He sprang into the air.

The mist grew dark, the crashing of the mountains grew distant, but the noise of the wind continued. Sparrow flew, dragging Kittel beside him, without knowing whether they were flying upwards or down, forwards or sideways. He flew to the very limit of his speed, but without being able to see anything to know how fast they were going. Kittel was whimpering Trina's name. Gradually they seemed to outstrip the dark wind, and light appeared somewhere ahead.

Slowly the light grew – the plain blue light of sky. And something else – dark, swirling shapes, that drew together into dark, hard shapes... And at last, a long mountain ridge with dark forests on its lower slopes, and below the forest, the shining surface of a lake.

A moment later they were standing on the shore. The trees pressed down almost to the edge of the lake, and mist moved amongst their silent trunks. The whole journey had been nothing but a tangled web of sorcery: they had scarcely travelled a mile from the Valley of Murmuring Water, and the sun of morning was still shining.

"It didn't happen," Sparrow said to Kittel, who stood blankly, pale and shivering. "We haven't been anywhere. It wasn't your sister."

Kittel was trembling too much to nod. "I thought she was too young," she managed between clenched teeth. "Trina's bound to have changed since I saw her, but she looked exactly the same as I remember her."

7

AT THE LAKE

"Kittel," Sparrow said urgently, "you didn't eat any of that white stuff, did you?"

"The sandwich? I spat it out – you saw me."

"You're quite sure?"

"Yes."

"I suppose you wouldn't be here if you had," Sparrow said. "We'd better get back."

"Back where?" Kittel asked, her voice firmer now.

"To the cottage," said Sparrow in surprise.

"Why?" Kittel frowned.

"Because – well – I don't know," Sparrow stumbled. "I suppose it can't be done – I suppose. . ."

"Do you think I'm going to let something like that stop me?" said Kittel. Her fright had left her angry.

"But how can we stop it happening?" Sparrow said. "We think we're doing fine and getting somewhere – and all the time we're just stuck in one place."

"It's obvious," said Kittel stubbornly. "We fly holding the stone. Everything disappears when you take it out; so if you have it out all the time nothing can go wrong."

Sparrow couldn't argue with this, but inwardly he was worrying more and more about Puckel.

"Come on," said Kittel. "I'm all right now. Let's not hang about any longer, or I'll never want to go."

And Sparrow let himself be persuaded.

Because he had to hold Kittel, they agreed that she should carry the stone, holding it out before them as they flew.

As they took to the air again, Kittel glanced back towards the ridge where the stream emerged from their own valley. "Isn't that Herold?" she exclaimed, pointing.

Sparrow hovered. There was a small dark shape visible against the rocky hillside, a black bird flapping along in an ungainly, haphazard fashion. No other bird flew quite as untidily as Herold.

"He'll have to be sent home," said Sparrow. "Perhaps the sight of us flying will send him into a huff."

"I don't know about that," said Kittel. "He's

coming straight towards us; he must have spotted us already."

Kittel was noticing a funny taste in her mouth. It seemed like the taste of blood, and she thought it must be from the little cut she had near her lip — perhaps from some spinning stone as the mountains crashed round them. Yet at the same time it seemed very sweet — sweeter than blood ought to be. "It's only the taste," she muttered to herself; "I definitely, definitely spat it out . . ."

By now Herold had come close enough for them to hear him. He was making the strangest noise — a sort of soft, crooning croak that sounded to Sparrow like, "Blind as a bat, blind as a bat".

Even with things happening so fast and so unexpectedly, Sparrow had a dim memory of Puckel telling him that one of the Polymorphs could strike people blind. Had Herold been attacked by the Polymorphs? Why should he be? All the same, it worried Sparrow.

"What's happened, Herold?" he called.

The crow switched direction slightly and headed straight for them, gibbering loudly about being abandoned in his hour of need.

"Hey! Look out!" Sparrow yelled, rising out of Herold's path. "You're going to knock into us!"

Sparrow turned, preparing to fly alongside Herold to find out what was wrong. But as he did so, Herold again altered course, apparently to follow the sound of Sparrow's voice. When Sparrow glanced back to see where his friend was, Herold was so close up behind them that Sparrow once again lost sight of him.

"Where's he gone now?" he exclaimed, lessening his speed; "where's – "

"Watch out, Herold, you – " Kittel burst out, suddenly aware that there would be a collision. "Don't – oh no!"

There was a bump and a fluttering, another yell from Kittel, a harsh caw and a soft plop from the lake below them. Herold was plummeting like a dropped bit of rag, before picking himself up just above the water, letting out a joyous squawk from which Sparrow understood that he could see again. Then Sparrow realized what Kittel had yelled.

"The stone?" he echoed. "Where? How?"

"There!" Kittel cried, almost in tears, pointing down to the rings spreading out on the calm surface of the water.

Sparrow didn't pause for a moment. Down he swooped, and would have plunged straight into the lake if Kittel hadn't stopped him with another shriek. Sparrow realized just in time, and straightened out, skimming over the surface.

He had to think quickly. "I'll leave you on the shore," he shouted. "But – I know. Herold, you fly round and round over those ripples, till I get back!" Without another word, he streaked off towards the shore, where he left Kittel standing forlornly in the shadow of the twisted trees.

When, a minute later, he had reached Herold again, he told the crow to go back and wait with Kittel. Then he dived down into the centre of what was now only the vaguest of vague, wide circles on the water face.

Sparrow was not the most expert of swimmers. But just as his dive had come to a slow stop and he was beginning to rise inexorably back to the surface, he noticed a fine, fat carp slithering off towards the weedy shadows.

Without a thought he took the fish's shape, and in his new fish-form swam nimbly back to where he thought he had been. It was lucky, for he was able to use the carp's unerring sense of direction under the water. In addition, Sparrow's shrunken mountain was a very special stone – he had looked after it night and day, treasured it, for eighteen months now; it had almost become a part of himself. He did not take long to find it sitting on a ledge of rock, and swam joyfully towards it.

And stopped, at a loss. Even before he had quite reached the stone he had realized the problem. For although the carp-shape had been ideal for finding it, the lippy, gaping fish mouth was nothing like big enough to lift it from its ledge. Sparrow swam round and round it, nudging it, kissing it with his fishy lips, sucking at it, clicking at it with his bony tongue.

Of course, the obvious thing would have been to change back into himself, grab the stone and float up to the surface. What stopped Sparrow was simple fear. In the heat of the moment he had been prepared to dive into the lake. Now he had calmed down. The fish-shape felt comfortable under the water, but the thought of being a boy so far below the surface horrified him. What if he found his lungs empty of air when he changed back into himself? He might simply drown, and no one ever know.

Sparrow was not a coward, but he needed a little time to think. He swam towards the surface. He had an idea that he would change into himself, take a reassuring gulp of air, then change back into the carp. Above his head, the light grew...

"Ow! Aagh!" Sparrow didn't exactly yell out loud, because fishes don't yell − but he yelled inside his head. A fearful pressure enveloped his neck and was crushing him, crushing out the cool feeling of breath in his shoulders, filling them with something else they had no right to be full of. A terrible, blinding warmth was around him, while something had pierced him through and through, something like great nails driven from one side of his body to the other.

He changed shape. It was automatic; he

didn't even know what shape he was changing into; he was simply saving his own life. Light was bubbling round his eyes, bubbling and breaking round his head. Instead of the languid, swift pushes of the carp's fins, he was propelling himself through the water at a great rate with powerful legs and arms, while a great, sidewards-swinging tail kept him on course. In his mouth was something sweet, something savoury, something that made his chops water and his stomach rumble in anticipation of a delicious feast!

The otter pulled itself on to the shore and dropped the fish, which twitched once and lay still. Sparrow changed into his own shape and looked down at the animal, which stared back up at him with black, unwinking eyes. No two otters could have that curious flash of yellow across their face...

"A partnership, the boy and Hnak," the otter said, glancing down at the fish. "The boy rides in the fish; Hnak clenches the fish; the boy rides in Hnak, safe back to the shore. The boy swims like an otter; Hnak feeds like a lion. What joy!" It looked down at the fish again, slavering.

Sparrow was confused at the otter. He realized, of course, that it was making him a sort of offer, but he was more taken up with wondering if it could really be the same one as he had met before. He knew by now that what most animals talked about, thought about, most of the time, was food — which was why the otter had seemed so unusual when it spoke to him after his encounter with the linden lady. Now it was talking — and behaving — like an ordinary otter. What did it know?

"Where's Kittel and Herold?" he burst out. He had got his bearings now. He was standing at the head of the lake, under the shadow of the cliff. And, gazing over to the point where he had left Kittel half an hour before, he saw the shore was empty. There was no doubt of it: the sun was shining brightly on the trees at the lakeside, and there was no one there.

"Your friends, the girl and the rag-bag crow?" The otter was unconcernedly grinding and slurping over its first mouthful of carp. "No hope for them, not ever now. Taken. Coils of mist, round and round, whispering and chuckling. Unprotected, they were. That stone..."

"I was trying to get the stone when you went and caught me!" Sparrow whispered weakly. For a moment, everything went black in front of his eyes. Crunch, crunch, slurp, crunch, went the otter at his feet. "Do you mean — the Polymorphs have captured them? Tell me!" he pleaded. "Will you please stop eating and tell me!"

The otter looked up in surprise. "Hnak can eat and talk together, all at once," it told Sparrow a little huffily. "Hnak can take you back to the stone, too. But no hurry: no hope. Drinking her own blood, the girl: no hope. On the way to the Labyrinth, and no getting out of there. Round and round, all the way in, and then round and round back out again, for ever."

8

SPELLBOUND

The Old Road shimmered in the hot sun; the mountains baked; the forests hummed and buzzed; the people of Copperhill and Villas were already complaining of the suffocating heat. "Too hot for June," were the words most often heard in either village.

Plato Smithers wasn't sure if it was anything to do with the heat, but things had become very sour in Copperhill. Ms Redwall didn't pester him any more, but he didn't have much chance to be glad of that. The reason she didn't pester him was because she simply did things without asking him now. Ms Redwall seemed to have grown over the past fortnight – even Plato Smithers felt small beside her now. There was something about her which he found a little alarming.

Not that everything was working out for her.

When she marched into the house next door and announced to Mariett Clodish – Lissie's mother – that she could now consider herself a free woman, her neighbour had simply cowered in a corner and trembled with fear. Her idea about the school didn't go too well either. When the children heard that Ms Redwall was to be the new teacher, they simply refused to go. She ordered their parents to make them go, but even that didn't work. "Let them have a summer holiday," people said. "It's too hot for school."

In the coolest place in the village, the wheel-room of the mill, Plato Smithers, still wearing his felt hat, stood with a small group of other men and sweated. Two of them, small wiry men with faces like wrinkled apples, were carrying crossbows and had quivers of bolts at their backs, along with heavy packs. Noddy Borrow and Cross Lurgan, two orchard keepers from the outskirts of the village, were preparing for a journey.

"Well, it's goodbye and good luck," Smithers said as he took each of them by the hand. "We know which way they've gone, though for sure we don't know how far they may be by now."

"We'll find them," said Noddy Borrow, who looked like a yellow apple. "Just you make sure and do your bit back here." Cross Lurgan, who looked like a red apple, nodded in agreement. "Put her in chains in the cellar, if need be," he said. "If she can do that to her own sister's boy, she can do it to anyone."

Gogs' father's idea had worked. When people heard that Ms Redwall's own nephew was among the ones who had left the village, it became the start of a secret attempt to get the woman under control. This was not easy, because although a number of people – including all the young people – were against her, she was continually holding meetings now and getting them whipped up about one thing or another, and in this way she still managed to get a lot of the people to think the same way as her.

None of the men meeting in the mill that day knew who had the worse job – the two who were to track Sparrow and his companions in the mountains, or the ones who had to stay behind and do something about Ms Redwall.

As the two men journeyed eastwards, a day's journey to the south of Copperhill the oak forests of Villas lay in stifling heat. Amongst the long lines of pillared trunks, Ormand's dog and the ball he had been chasing had both got lost, and Lissie was getting very short-tempered as they searched for them.

"What's wrong with you?" Ormand said.

"Nothing! Obviously!" Lissie stormed, giving him a filthy look and flouncing off through the chest-high ferns.

"He didn't go that way!" Ormand called after her. He was trying to remain good-tempered, but somehow he felt angry at her being so angry — after all, it wasn't anybody's fault. Lissie ignored him and continued out of sight between the still trunks of the oak forest. He made a face and went after her.

He thought she might have cooled down a bit by the time he came up with her, but the moment she saw him she burst out again: "I hate the flies here! I can't stand them! They're everywhere!"

A cloud of flies was certainly buzzing determinedly round her; but to Ormand it didn't seem worse than flies at any other time in bracken-filled woods. "They're round me too," he pointed out.

"Oh, you — yes, I can see they're round you," she spat back. "But you wouldn't even notice! You're used to them!"

"Don't you have flies in your woods, then?" he asked, with just a hint of mockery in his voice.

"No, we don't!"

"Not a single one?"

"No!"

"Huh," Ormand said. "You were probably never allowed to go out of your garden, that's why — in case you got your clothes dirty!"

Lissie flew at him. She attacked him like a wildcat and a donkey rolled into one —

scratched him with her hands and kicked him with her feet. It was the most vicious attack Ormand had ever experienced. He was bigger and stronger than she, but even so it was only by luck that he managed to topple her over a tussock of grass and hold her down.

At that moment the dog, Boffin, suddenly returned with a rush and a crash. He stood at the edge of the bracken, looking at them, legs slightly splayed, panting. Lissie relaxed. Ormand released his hold on her.

"It was all your fault," Ormand told him. "Why did you run off? What got into you?"

Whatever had got into him was still there. Boffin suddenly began to bark at them; excitedly, sharply, persistently.

"Be quiet!" Ormand yelled. But the barking went on.

"I think he must have found something," Lissie said quietly.

Ormand scrambled to his feet. "Not the ball, anyway. Come on, boy. Show us!"

Boffin swung round and went bounding off through the bracken again. Lissie got up, and quickly they followed his trail through the listening aisles of the forest. A couple of times they lost track of him, but each time he came back, bounding and barking, then whisking round and careering off again.

"These flies are getting worse," Lissie said disbelievingly. Even Ormand had to admit they were troublesome now. They buzzed and buzzed, so close to their heads that they could feel their faces flicked occasionally by the insects' wings.

At last they heard Boffin ahead, squeaking, whining, letting out little jabbing barks. There were more and more flies: the whole air seemed dark with them, and the buzzing of their thousands of wings seemed to fill the whole forest and throb in their ears like drums.

Boffin was leaping and scratching round something in the grass. The flies seemed to be thickest round it. It almost looked as though they were pouring upwards from it.

"Ugh!" Lissie exclaimed, turning away. "It's something dead!" But something made Ormand go on further, to shoo the flies out of the way and get a closer look.

"Lissie, come quickly," he said.

Reluctantly she came to his side. It was a dead animal; a smallish dog. Lissie saw at once why Ormand looked so dumbfounded; apart from a red gash in its side, the dog matched Boffin in every detail. It had Boffin's unusual white patch between the eyes, the same black pad on its left forepaw. There was something about it, dull and lifeless though it was, which simply *was* Boffin. If Boffin hadn't been leaping around in front of their very eyes, they would most certainly have believed that Ormand's dog was dead. And all the while the flies buzzed and thrummed, thrummed and throbbed, in the still air of the oak forest. Both children stared helplessly at the dead creature at their feet, but neither bent to touch it or turned away to leave it. They seemed mesmerized by it, rooted to the spot — spellbound.

Several hours later a search party, consisting of Lissie's father, Ormand's uncle and a couple of neighbours, followed Boffin up into the oak forest. They could find no trace of the two missing children. Some broken bracken stems led to a spot where rabbit fur and a rabbit paw were lying in a small, flattened patch of grass — but otherwise, there was nothing.

It was Boffin who roused Ormand and Lissie again — or perhaps "roused" is the wrong word. Something had happened to them; something had changed inside them. They were still aware of what was happening, but somehow it had all become very distant, as if it were a story from long ago.

Boffin was barking again, excitedly and urgently, as if to get them to follow him. The flies buzzed and buzzed. Suddenly he turned and again went rocketing off into the woods. They stirred, looked round, but before they had even had time to think of moving, the dog appeared again, trotting smartly off *away* from them as if he had only that second left the side of the dead dog. So of course he couldn't have appeared again — this must be another Boffin. But which was the real one? The one which had crashed off through the trees, the dead one, or the one trotting off ahead of them now? They followed this last.

Some way further on, the Boffin they were following stopped and sniffed in the long grass. There was another dead Boffin, lying in the shadow of a thicket of young trees. Again the same thing happened: as they looked, Boffin ran off with a yelp into the woods; Boffin lay dead at their feet; Boffin trotted quietly off ahead of them, leading them further into the forest. And they followed. They had stopped wondering, or even thinking, by now. Five times this same scene was re-enacted.

"Where are we, Ormand?" Lissie asked an hour later.

"I don't know," Ormand replied dully.

And suddenly they were out of the forest — on a broad, dreary stretch of moorland that lay between two parts of it. The summer day seemed to have gone; the land lay under a light like a dull evening of autumn. Large rocks were scattered here and there in the heather and rough grass, and Boffin made his way purposefully amongst them.

With a yelp and a howl, the five missing Boffins reappeared. They popped out from behind various rocks, all at once, and began a mad chase, in and out, backwards and forwards, over tussocks, over stones, crossing and recrossing the moor – until suddenly all five of them converged on the one Boffin Lissie and Ormand were following: converged all at once, with breathtaking speed, six dogs becoming one dog.

"Boffin!" Ormand called out, his voice itself sounding sharp as a dog's yelp. As if in answer, the dog did a head over heels, and by the time Lissie and Ormand came up to him, a sixth dead dog lay in the wiry moorland grass. For a moment they stood and stared down. Then softly Ormand bent to touch the still head.

Wowf! The very second he did so, with a leap and a bound that sent him tumbling backwards, one, two, three . . . five . . . ten Boffins leaped out of the dead Boffin. Like a hunting pack they went jostling and streaming off towards the forest on the far side of the moor. And Ormand and Lissie followed, running, running, running till their breath came in gasps and their legs ached and their lungs felt like bursting.

Closer the forest loomed, and closer again, but it seemed to take an age to reach it. At last they understood why: it was more distant than it had seemed, and the trees of it were oaks three times – six times – as large as any oak trees they had ever seen. Nightmarishly huge they loomed up in the dull sky, and in the roots of the hugest, at the edge of the forest, an immense rabbit hole gaped like an open mouth. They did not hesitate. By now the yelping of the hounds had faded away ahead of them, but they were scarcely up to the forest eaves when it broke out suddenly behind them. Behind them and drawing nearer. They were being hunted . . .

They dived into the rabbit hole and ran, as all sound faded behind them. They slowed to a walk, then stopped, gasping to get their breath back. There was a velvety silence behind the noise they were making – but behind the silence the ghost of another noise: perhaps a faint whirring, like a flock of pigeons just taking flight. They were completely enclosed in the tunnel, with no trace of an entrance either before or behind them. Yet they were able to see, in a dim, brownish light like a faint echo of the dreary light they had come in from.

"There's no reason why we should be able to see in here," Ormand remarked presently. "If we really were in a tunnel under the ground, it'd be pitch black; we wouldn't see a thing."

"I'm scared," said Lissie. It was the first thing she had said since they found the second dead dog. "I feel dizzy," she added.

"And yet we are underground," Ormand went on after a little, "because this is earth, and these are tree roots sticking out of it. Look." He pulled at a fibrous end and drew an unmistakable tree root from the crumbling tunnel wall. Right up the wall and round the roof he pulled it, as a gentle rain of earth fell on their hair.

"Be careful," Lissie warned. "You'll bring the whole tunnel down."

But Ormand went on pulling, and the root kept on coming. Over the roof, slanting down the opposite wall, and across the floor –

"Ormand!" Lissie cried out – a split second before, with a gentle pitter-patter, then a soft, choking *sumph!*, the tunnel collapsed, crushing them to their knees with the soft weight of earth.

They went down without a sound, too surprised to cry out. A moment later they were able to struggle to their feet again, barely up to their knees in earth. Then Lissie smeared the soil out of her eyes – and let out a loud scream: framed in the loose earth of the collapsed wall was a frightful, wrinkled, leering face.

"No need to be scared." The thin-lipped mouth moved in an unnatural, automatic fashion as the grinding stony voice came from it. Pieces of earth could be seen falling from it in the gloom as it spoke. "No need to be scared. I'm here to welcome you in."

Then the head detached itself from the wall, and Lissie and Ormand saw a skinny, brown-clad body with long, bony arms, and in one hand a lantern in which flickered a tiny, chocolate-coloured flame. The flame cast no light, but somehow the look of it was the same as the brown gloom that filled the earthy tunnel. "I've come to let you in through the door," the creature croaked.

"What door?" Ormand demanded in a shaky voice.

"Why, this door," the voice grated. And they saw the plain wooden boards of a door where the tunnel wall had been.

"Where does it go?" Lissie whispered.

"Why, it says here on the door, child. Can't you read it?"

"There's nothing there," said Lissie, staring at the door.

"Look," the lantern bearer rasped, with a black, hollow grin. "It's written on the door. A – M – A –" the bony finger moved across the plain wood of the door as the dry mouth spelled out letters – "Z – E – M – E – N – T. What does that say?"

"I don't know," Lissie replied.

"It says Amazement!" the ancient mouth roared, as the door burst open in another shower of earth. "IT SAYS AMAZEMENT!" The empty doorway seemed to do a cartwheel towards them. "*It says Amazement!*" came a third time, muffled now and echoing and mixed with the slamming sound of wood on wood on the "maze" sound. Lissie and Ormand stood alone in a squared corridor of rock, beside a flickering torch fixed into a bracket on the wall.

And then there was silence, apart from the frenzied thumping of their hearts. Gradually they grew calmer, and noticed there was something oddly peaceful about the place they were in. They looked about them. The corridor was wide, with walls of rough sandstone, clean and dry. At about twice their height there was an arched ceiling of bare earth. In contrast, the floor was of smooth, polished stone flags that gleamed a little with a deep reddish tinge like garnet rock. There was a slight curve to the walls of the corridor, and the torchlight reached just far enough for them to see where it curved out of sight. The torch flame sputtered now and then, giving off a bluish, honey-scented smoke.

"I wonder what keeps them lighted?" said Ormand, who had noticed that the brackets, and the torches themselves, were of stone and bore no trace of the usual material − pitch or tallow − that torches burn on.

Lissie didn't like the thought of torches with no fuel to keep them alight. What was to stop them going out at any moment? "What do we do?" she said. There was no sign of any door now. Where they stood the corridor ended − or started − in a blank stone wall.

"Go on, I suppose. We can't stay here."

They started down the corridor.

"It seems a bit boring, this place," Lissie said when after a while they came to a second, and then a third torch on the wall.

It was true. The passage seemed to go on forever, with nothing happening — no doors, no rooms — just more passageway, all exactly the same, gently, monotonously, continuously curving out of sight ahead. The torches sputtered on the wall, quite far apart, but never far enough apart for anywhere to be in complete darkness. They had already gone a good way, and Lissie had just counted two hundred and forty steps between one torch and the next, when —

"Did you hear a voice?" she whispered.

"No," Ormand replied, stopping. "But I thought I saw something moving, on ahead — away from us."

"What shall we do?" Lissie whispered.

"Keep behind me, close to the wall," Ormand whispered back. We'll run and catch up. Tiptoe."

They didn't have far to run, and when they suddenly came in view of the next torch they stopped, quite baffled. Kittel was sitting beneath it, with a large crow on her shoulder.

9

INTO THE SPIRAL

Kittel's smile was friendly as they came up to her. But Lissie immediately had the feeling there was something amiss.

"Hello," Kittel said, without any surprise in her voice. "Hello."

The crow on Kittel's shoulder stuck its head out and hissed, so Lissie didn't go right up to her friend. "Do you know where we are?" she asked, after a pause.

"Ye – es," said Kittel slowly. But instead of telling Lissie, she asked, "How did you get here?"

Lissie told her. She had a feeling that Kittel was only half listening, and when she had finished, Kittel just remarked, in a reassuring sort of voice, "Yes, dogs are like that, really. But there's nothing you can do about it; you just have to take them as they are."

"Kittel, are you all right?" Lissie asked anxiously.

Kittel gave a short laugh. "It's that stuff I took," she said vaguely. "It's just like ordinary bread to taste, really, but you get hooked on it. It's all this junk food, it's stuffed full of chemicals and you don't know what half of them are doing to you. Trina, could you turn that radio down a bit, please?" Suddenly she seemed to notice Ormand. She got up immediately and held out her hand to him. "Oh, hello, you must be Sparrow." She said it in the same unnatural, over-polite way that Lissie's mother had when she spoke to Ms Redwall.

"Its Ormand, Kittel," Lissie pleaded, now thoroughly worried. "I told you about him. Ormand," she said, turning to him, "there's something wrong with her – she's not like this."

"Kittel's told me so much about you," Kittel said confidingly to Ormand. "Can you really fly? It must be *so* exciting!"

"She's gone mad," Lissie whispered; "she's completely lost her head. Oh no, not another one – what'll we do?"

"She is a bit odd," Ormand agreed.

"Now," Kittel said, and her voice had changed again; she spoke in clear, slow tones, like a teacher addressing a rather dull class, "it's really much easier than it looks. Now, pay attention to the map." She turned to the wall and ran her finger over a part of it. "The red arrow helps you. It says YOU ARE HERE – so you can't really go wrong. Trina, take those headphones off – you have to pay attention." (She glanced severely at Lissie as she said this.) "You know the name of the street you want to go to, but you don't know where it is. Now down here there's a list of street names, in alphabetical order, and after each street name there's a letter and a number. Now, look along the side of the map . . ."

"What are we going to do?" Lissie whispered again.

"I don't know," Ormand whispered back. "Humour her, I suppose."

"And it's . . . this way!" Kittel announced. "Come on!" And she turned and started smartly down the passageway, the crow on her shoulder teetering backwards and forwards with each step she took.

Lissie and Ormand exchanged glances, and then set off after her.

It would not have been too bad if it hadn't been for Kittel. Lissie had long since decided that, wherever they were, it wasn't a horrific place to be in, considering the horror of the doorway into it. The floor was smooth and pleasant to walk on and the passage was never too dark, because of the sweet-smelling torches – even though they did cast rather eerie shadows on the silent, honey-coloured walls. But the constant stream of nonsense coming from Kittel was distressing; especially since she kept changing her voice, and never appeared to be any one particular person for more than half a minute at a time. Through that endless-seeming, torchlit journey, Lissie heard her talking like her mother, like Ms Minn, like herself, like Sparrow, like Sparrow's mother, like some other teacher, like Plato Smithers – and Lissie even recognized herself when Kittel suddenly put out her hand and sang:

Hedgehog, hedgehog, down by the well,
Find me a snail with a curly shell.

In the middle of giving a long lecture to Sparrow about not having cut enough firewood, she suddenly said, "Oh, Dad, you're always hiding behind that newspaper"; in the middle of throwing a stick for her dog, and then pelting off after it as though she were a dog herself (the crow fell off and had to fly along behind her), she suddenly burst into tears and announced, "I have to go away now, dears, and I'm afraid I might never see you again."

All this time a gradual change was taking place in the passageway. For a while they didn't notice it, then Lissie first and Ormand not long afterwards commented on it. The curve of the walls had become much sharper. And the reason they hadn't noticed sooner was that the torches were set closer together. Ormand measured the distance with his feet: there were only sixty steps between them.

Lissie was softly repeating her rhyme about the hedgehog and the snail. "I know," she said suddenly, "it's a spiral. Like a snail shell."

"What is?" said Ormand.

"What we're in," she answered. "When we get to the centre, it'll stop."

"Oh, Trina, *please* turn that radio down," Kittel broke in.

And in the small silence after she had spoken, they heard a voice.

It was a soft, murmuring, distinct voice, floating easily along the passage towards them, though without words that they could make out. But they only had a second in which to listen to it, because the crow suddenly burst into such a cacophony of caws and screeches and flappings of its wings that Lissie automatically flung herself against the wall, covering her head with her arms.

The silence returned after a moment or two – a silence without any sound of the voice. Lissie uncovered her head. Kittel was wagging her finger at some small, invisible person in front of her. "Tut, tut, tut," she was saying. "That's what happens when you don't do up your shoelaces." There was no sign of the crow.

"What happened?" said Lissie.

"The crow flew off," Ormand said. "Don't ask me why."

"Where?" asked Lissie.

"On ahead," Ormand answered.

After some tense listening, they went on again. There didn't seem anything else to do, and besides, they felt they should keep Kittel in sight. Lissie seemed to be right: the curve of the passageway was very definitely tightening. "Only thirty steps between the torches now," said Ormand.

They paced out the distances together: twenty-five – twenty-three – eighteen – seventeen – and stopped. For about twenty steps the corridor ran on ahead of them and then came to an end in a blank wall. There was one last torch just before it. And the moment they came in sight of the end of the corridor, they heard the voice again.

It was a man's voice, it seemed, though murmuring in a rather high, chant-like fashion, like someone trying to remember a poem by repeating it over and over. But it was no poem the voice was repeating; in fact, it seemed to be plain nonsense.

"Ngamawa cumarana baranaia wumawanga," it murmured, quietly, continuously as a stream bubbling to itself in a shady hollow under the trees. It was right ahead of them, but they could see nothing.

Almost nothing, that is. For on to the floor

against the wall opposite the torch, a small black something suddenly flopped – almost as though it had jerked itself out of the wall. It became still. It looked very like the wing of a bird.

Kittel didn't hesitate. "Just coming!" she called gaily and trotted off towards the torch and the thing on the floor. Lissie and Ormand followed.

They caught up with her just as they came to the black thing. It was the crow, which lay, either dead or senseless, in a stone doorway in the wall of the passage. Kittel gave the creature no more than a glance. "Trina," she remarked, "I've told you a dozen times not to leave your underwear lying about," and she advanced through the doorway. Lissie and Ormand were right behind her, and this, and the huge dancing shadows thrown on the wall by the torchlight, meant that they didn't at first see what was in the small, circular chamber they were entering.

When they did, they froze in shock, and Lissie clapped her hand over her mouth.

It was a chamber of rough stone, just like the corridor. In the centre of it stood a round stone table. Just beside the table there was a tripod of some black metal, its three legs meeting at the top and then curling back into a sort of collar of wrought ironwork. Sticking out of the centre of the collar was a spike, and fixed to the spike there was the head of a man.

The dark face was towards them, and the dark eyes were closed or lowered. The face looked utterly peaceful; and the murmuring stream of meaningless sounds was coming from its scarcely moving lips. "Ngathaiathaia rumalinea bumarinoyo haikanaragaia brandulimotho moronigora," it intoned.

Kittel was already advancing towards it. "Oh, you must be Sparrow's father," she exclaimed, holding out her hand. "I'm so glad to have met you at last – I've heard so much about you."

10

DOORS IN THE EARTH

The otter was difficult to persuade. Even after it had finished its fish it didn't seem to feel much urgency about Sparrow's problem. Kittel and Herold, as far as it was concerned, were gone; nothing anyone could do would bring them back. It was sad, but life had to go on and fish had to be caught.

It *was* the same otter Sparrow had met before, and it remembered Sparrow quite well, but it remembered nothing about the mysterious message it had given him. It knew of Puckel (Who doesn't? it said), but it couldn't see how Puckel could help; Puckel had left the mountains hundreds of years ago. Nothing Sparrow said could persuade it otherwise.

Eventually it accepted that its scheme for catching fish was too dangerous for Sparrow, and by this time anyway its hunger was well satisfied. It belched a few times, said that had been the best carp it had ever tasted, and agreed to take Sparrow back to the place where it had caught the fish.

Its sense of direction was unfailing, and with its guidance and then a change into a second carp, which Sparrow made sure didn't swim up towards the surface, he found his way back to his stone a second time. Not knowing what else to do, he changed into it, and waited and thought, though not one idea came to him about rescuing Kittel and Herold from the Labyrinth of the Polymorphs – wherever, whatever, that was. Apart from this, his conscience was badly nagging him: he should have gone back to see Puckel. If he had, he wouldn't be in this mess now.

Time moves differently for stones. He had scarcely decided that the best way of helping Kittel would be to go to Puckel, when he realized by the turning spiral of silver that he was already on the way. That meant it must be night-time and he must have been on the lake bed for hours.

Things were different this time. There was no road of mist. And after a little, he realized that the silver spiral was actually becoming clearer, sharper, smaller. It stopped circling. It was a small, silver brooch, just in front of Sparrow's eyes, and –

It was the brooch on Puckel's magnificent

midnight-blue cloak! Sparrow was inside the tower!

"Puckel," he said, "we're in trouble now."

"No doubt you are!" Puckel retorted. "And no wonder. Do you think I've nothing better to do than walk up and down this room, while you picnic and skylark in the mountains?" The old man's hair flew wildly as he stomped this way and that across the bare stone floor.

Sparrow felt a little indignant at having two of the hardest-working weeks of his life referred to as skylarking and picnicking, but it seemed the wrong time to argue about it. "Puckel, Kittel—" he began.

"Don't Puckel-Kittel me!" Puckel snapped. "Attend. The Vault of the Bear no longer offers any protection. The noose draws in. Already the Polymorphs are striking towards the Centre."

Sparrow did not dare to interrupt.

"The strategy is this," Puckel continued. "Bur of the Lamps, their head, has set Eych the Enslaver to guard the source of their power, which is in the Star Wheel itself; Ur is set to guard the perimeters; Eni, Tho and Yo to dim the light of Cold Stone as siege is laid about Hollywell – there is duplication of forms, shapes and shadows in the forest, danger to all who stray from the villages, danger reaching into the heart of the villages, evil from the outside meeting with evil in the

133

hearts of fools. Drakewater, Uplands and the Springing Wood are safe for the present, though not for long if the Centre is endangered. Bur goes among them, unseen, holding them to his will. Bur is the key. Bur must be provoked, brought out into the open. Is that clear?"

Sparrow shook his head. He had not even begun to understand.

Puckel stopped, frowned, sighed, folded his hands over the top of his stick and tapped his foot. "Well, what's so difficult?" he demanded.

"Everything," Sparrow said. "All these names. The names of the Polymorphs, and the names of the villages, and the names of these other things, and the Star Wheel and the Vault of the Bear – I just don't know what you're talking about, that's all."

"You've seen the Door, haven't you?" Puckel said, now tapping his stick on the floor as well as his foot.

"What door?" said Sparrow.

"Why, the door you came through, of course!" the old man exploded.

Sparrow glanced round. Had he come in by a door? Apparently he had. There seemed to be no window in Puckel's room now, but where the window had been there was an empty doorway. Through it nothing was visible but black space and brilliant stars. But Sparrow scarcely noticed that; the door itself was what took his attention. It was identical to the strange-shaped doorway of the cottage.

He turned round again and found that Puckel had somehow got up on the little wooden table, where he was precariously perched with his legs tucked under him. There was no sign of his stick.

"I shall explain," said Puckel. "I might as well, or we'll just be plagued by your stupid interruptions. Listen carefully.

"A long time ago − so many years I wouldn't care to count them, years before memory − this world was still in the making. In those days, giants were here. Not the sorry creatures of the nursery tales you're all so fond of down there. These were real giants, out-topping the highest mountains, their shoulders above the clouds. They were the craftsmen, and the mountains and valleys and seas were their handicraft. Well, that's all long gone; their time passed before memory began.

"But they didn't leave the earth − no, they built themselves doors in it and went down below, down to the centre. Mountains slipped and seas washed over the lands, new hills were carved by rivers of ice; the giants' doors were buried. But they are all still there, and where they are discovered, a great power of making and unmaking, of hiding and revealing, can be set loose. This whole mountain-country is such a place."

"Where − you mean . . ." Sparrow faltered.

"I mean the country you call your country, this lost country of mountains, with its five ridiculous little villages. They're all inside the frame of one of the giants' doors. A five-sided frame, exactly like this one and the one you've seen before."

"But huge," Sparrow murmured. "It must be huge."

"Huge enough," said Puckel, "though you could cross it in a single day – indeed you used to, before you started using that tomfool of a crow as your permanent conveyance. However, the size doesn't matter. What has happened with the Giants' Door is that it has been used to make the Secret Way of the Mountains.

"The Giants' Door is like a broken mirror: when a mirror is broken, each fragment is a little mirror of its own. There are nine hundred and ninety-nine doors; each of these is the Giants' Door in miniature. They are all one door. So anyone who has mastered the Secret Way can move faster than thought between door and door. To learn the Secret Way he must first see through the illusions of the Polymorphs and then chain them to his service. Thus he becomes a master of transformation."

Sparrow didn't feel much wiser for this explanation, but Puckel didn't ask him this time if he had understood. "Now," the old man went on, "you've gone and dumped your friend Kittel and that black scraggle of feathers in the maze of the Polymorphs, and they're no use to me there. Those two young well-keepers are in there too, though that's no fault of yours.

"However, as I want you to learn the Secret Way, these matters will sort themselves out in due course."

"Can I not help them?" said Sparrow.

"No. What you must do for me will help them."

"And what's that?"

"You must go to the Vault of the Bear," said Puckel, "and discover what stone thing the Polymorphs have taken from it. Then you must go to the Star Wheel and find it."

"How do I get to the Vault of the Bear?"

"By the Secret Way."

"But I don't know it."

"Exactly. Because you have been wasting time."

Sparrow at last began to see things from Puckel's point of view. "Do you mean I can't help Kittel and Herold till I learn the Secret Way?" he said.

"Exactly," said Puckel again.

"What about my stone? I can beat the Polymorphs with that."

"Oh, can you?" said Puckel drily. "Then why are you sitting at the bottom of a lake?"

Sparrow was silent.

"Well, well," said Puckel, "it's not the end of the world. Now, listen. There is a place of power in each angle of the great Door. The Vault of the Bear and the Star Wheel are such places. They are hidden, and they can only be reached by someone who has learned the Secret Way. Such a person can, on occasion, open the door between them and the world of everyday. On occasion, though it can be risky – "

He broke off, and stared down at Sparrow's arm.

Sparrow followed his gaze. Wrapped round the arm from wrist to elbow – like a snake, but quite definitely no snake – was Puckel's stick! Polished and gnarled, Sparrow recognized it at once, though how it had been possible for that hard, dry piece of wood to coil itself round his arm like ivy round a tree, Sparrow could not begin to think. He stared for a moment, then looked up and stared at Puckel.

"Well, you couldn't have made it much clearer than that," the old man grumbled. He was speaking to the stick, not to Sparrow. "Not much for me to say, then. She'll teach you what you need to know. None too gently, I'm afraid, but all the quicker for that – and quick is what we need to be now."

"You said I had to find a missing bit of me first," said Sparrow.

"You already have," said Puckel carelessly, "or pretty nearly. Now, go and get on. And when your work has all been done, then throw the water into the sun. Then all join hands, with

138

a wink and a grin, and shout like mad when the drums begin."

Sparrow gazed at the old man. "That was like Lissie's rhyme," he said wonderingly. "How did you know it?"

"Same way as she knew it," Puckel answered, sticking his finger into his ear. "By listening." He stuck a finger into his other ear, screwed his eyes shut, and pursed his mouth. He was like a figure carved out of stone.

"Time to go," said a harsh voice from Sparrow's wrist. "Haven't you wasted enough time already?"

It was the stick speaking, and without waiting for a reply it gently tugged at Sparrow's arm, and he drifted out through the doorway and into the night of stars, along the road of mist.

"I thought it was something to do with my father, when Puckel said there was a part of me missing," Sparrow said as they went.

"Your thoughts are like mud in a sump," the stick replied. "You stir them up and your mind becomes clouded. Let them go."

Sparrow took a deep breath. "What do we do, then?"

"Rise," the stick grated.

"Rise where?" Sparrow asked.

"Up to the air," the stick crackled. "Do you want to drown?"

"I can't drown here," Sparrow said, "there's

no wa – oh! Blub!"

He kicked, struggled, panicked, breathless...

Writhing, rising...

And with a crash of breaking water, they were in the air again. Sparrow took great thankful gulps of it as, still, they shot upwards, slowed down and hovered.

He was in full, warm sunlight, with the little pyramid of rock clutched painfully in his hand. Below lay the long, narrow, tree-girt lake. Over the stony ridge he could see down to the little cottage in the Valley of Murmuring Water.

"I always seem to end up here," Sparrow remarked.

"This is where you started," the stick said. "Come."

Sparrow swooped downwards, but when they had entered the valley, the stick pulled him away from the cottage, and they landed in the new-mown hay beside the stream. He struggled to put the stone back in his pouch, which was difficult because of the stick round his arm. Then he looked about. There was no sign of life anywhere. "Where are Gogs and Murie?" he asked.

"Prisoners," the stick replied curtly.

"Not – in the Labyrinth too?"

"In themselves," said the stick. "Like most human creatures. It is little different from being in the maze of the Polymorphs. All you need know is that the boy is beating rocks together and singing love songs to the goat—"

"What? Gogs?" Sparrow exclaimed, but the stick paid no heed.

"That is the work of the Polymorph Ur, though it is possible you would prefer to think of the creature as the lady of linden blossom." There was something about the way the stick said this which made Sparrow go pink with embarrassment.

"Where's Murie?" he asked quickly.

"The woman is riding on the back of the cow down in the wood," the stick replied.

Sparrow gasped.

"She has twined flowers in its horns and carries a leafy sceptre," it went on drily. "Now attend. In all that concerns the Secret Way of the Mountains, the speaking of names is of importance. Names are what hold a thing together. When the time comes, you will find that the cottage is an island of safety. Touch the left-hand doorpost and speak the names of the woman and the boy, then they will come back and be as much themselves as they have ever been. Now cross the stream."

The stream was a little too wide to jump at this point, but considering the imperious mood of the stick – it had given his arm a sharp tug as it spoke – Sparrow didn't dare to waste time looking for a spot where it was narrower. The water, cold even on the warm summer day, swirled strongly round his shins.

"Stop," the stick ordered, before he had quite reached the far bank. He stopped, and waited. The swirling water began to give him a queer, trembly feeling in his legs – almost as if they were turning to water themselves. He glanced over towards the wood, to see if there were any sign of Murie and the cow. There was none. Higher the feeling mounted in his legs . . .

"Stick me into the ground," said the stick suddenly.

"How?" he asked. "I can't even get you off my arm."

"Straighten yourself out, then you'll manage," it replied.

"What?" said Sparrow, frowning.

Next instant, the whole world seemed to turn inside out. Not only Sparrow's arm, but his whole body – not only his body, but everything round him, the stream, the grass, the wood, the mountains, the sky, seemed to twist itself into one vast corkscrew-shape. It was ridiculous, sickening, dizzying. The only straight thing in the whole world seemed to be the stick. A moment later everything had returned to normal, and there was the stick, straightened out – as much as it ever could be – in Sparrow's hand. Hurriedly he leaned over and stuck it into the soft ground of the bank.

"The Secret Way is like the stick on your arm," said the stick. "You thought your arm

142

was straight and the stick was twisted round it. In fact the stick was straight, and you were twisted. The Secret Way is the straight way, but it touches on every part of the mountains. The mountains are crooked, the Way is straight. It is the quickest and truest way."

"Yes," said Sparrow.

"Yesss," the stick hissed back at him, seeming to bend towards him from the bank. "And now you will learn to see."

Sparrow had seen it happen before, but it never failed to surprise him. The stick was bending, was becoming pliable; brown and red coils were lying on the ground, writhing, until with a soft *thluck!* a tail jerked itself out of the ground. The stick had become a snake.

Sparrow stood in the water, gazing at what had been dry wood and was now living creature. Stick handle was now snake's head, and the raised head came closer, closer. A sensation like fear crept through Sparrow, trembling and weak as he already was from the water. Yet it was not like the fear that makes you shrink away, cower in a corner, or even run. Indeed as the snake bent towards him, it seemed that he was also bending towards it. Its eyes seemed to be shining, so that they made a circle of gold light all round its head. Its head, black in the midst of the circle, came closer still, grew larger, swayed from side to side, as though searching for something in each of his eyes in turn.

Sparrow watched, fascinated, as the thin black tongue flickered in and out. Then all at once the snake drew back its lips, bared its fangs, and struck. With a cry, Sparrow clutched at his left eye and fell backwards, gurgling into the stream as the water closed over his head.

11

OUT OF THE COILS

Seeing her friend about to try and shake hands with a head that had no body was enough for Lissie. With a scream of "Kittel!" she launched herself across the circular chamber and grabbed Kittel by the shoulders before she had reached the stone table.

"Trina! Not here!" Kittel hissed at her through her teeth, trying to free herself. But Lissie hung on for dear life. The more Kittel struggled, the more Lissie held on, until, tripping on a leg of the table, they lost their balance and both landed sprawled on the floor, Kittel on top.

They would have gone on struggling, if it hadn't been for the crow.

The crow was lying just in front of their noses. Lissie had barely hit the floor when the bird's still body gave a jerk and then a heave.

One wing flapped, and then the beak opened. But what came out of the crow's beak was not a crow's voice; it was the deep, quiet voice of a man.

"Be still," the crow's beak said. "There's nothing to fear."

Lissie and Kittel grew quite still, and gaped. Ormand, standing in the doorway, gaped.

"The crow is unharmed," the voice went on. "It has only knocked itself senseless. Through it, I can speak to you. Listen: I am what you have come to find."

Kittel's eyes ranged round the chamber in a vague sort of way. It was Lissie who answered the crow. "You can't be," she blurted, "because we're not looking for anything. We — we got lost in here, and we're trying to get out."

"No, stupid," Kittel interrupted, heaving herself up from on top of Lissie and looking not at the crow but straight at the head. "It was Dad we were trying to find — that was the whole point in going."

Lissie was still staring at the crow, but Ormand looked towards the head as Kittel spoke to it. He distinctly saw the lips smile on the peaceful face.

"I think you've got a beautiful face," Kittel told the head. "Now that we've found you, what should we do?"

The head smiled again. "You must go back

out," the crow's beak stated in the man's voice.

"We don't know if we can," Ormand put in. "You see, we were shut into this maze thing – we think it's a spiral – by someone. They wanted —"

"They wanted you to be lost in amazement," the man's voice interrupted gently. "But it is not what they shall have. You will keep your feet on the ground – to that extent I can help you. Go now."

And suddenly Herold gave a great jerk, then a great sigh. His eye opened and for a moment glared up at Lissie, who scrambled to her feet and backed away. But Herold flapped his wing free of the wall and flew up to the roof of the small room with a loud squawk of bird invective. Then he flew down and perched on Lissie's head; she clung to Ormand and rolled her eyes distrustfully upwards, but didn't try to remove the uninvited guest.

"But Dad!" Kittel exclaimed. "We've come all this way to find you! You're not going to make us go away again?"

"Ngaio ngomo ignomo naiarabaranara," the head intoned senselessly, out of its own mouth now.

They listened to the stream of wordless sounds for a few seconds more, and then –

"I want you to come with us," Kittel declared.

"What – that?" Lissie squeaked, swinging

round towards her friend and flapping her hand towards the head. "You can't touch *that*!" Then – "Ow!" for her sudden movement had made the crow grip tightly on to her head to keep his balance.

"Yes," Kittel replied determinedly. "We've come all this way, and honestly I don't like going on the Underground at the best of times with all those strange people about, so I don't see why we should have a wasted journey."

"It's not your dad, Kittel!" Lissie cried, almost in tears. "It's just a head on a spike – it's horrible."

Kittel stared stupidly through her. It was impossible to tell if she'd even heard what Lissie had said.

Fright was making Lissie angry. "Well, I'm not staying with you if you've got it," she said fiercely. "I'm going."

"We really should stay together you know, Lissie," Ormand said, though his voice was trembling. "It's not very nice in here."

"I know that," Lissie flashed back at him, "so I don't see why we should try to make it nastier!" And she turned round to leave the chamber.

But Kittel seemed as determined as Lissie. By the time Lissie had stepped out into the passageway (Herold still gripping doggedly to her head), she had crossed the room again, skirted the stone table, and was within reach of the head on its tripod. Ormand remained where he had been, unable to decide whether to follow Lissie or stay with Kittel. Lissie continued on her way, and by the time Kittel reached out to the head, murmuring, "Come on, Dad, don't mind Trina," Lissie was out of Ormand's sight.

But even Lissie, out in the passageway, stopped dead when Kittel touched the head. And Ormand, who was neither coming nor going, clapped his hands over his ears and let himself sink into a huddle on the floor.

What happened when Kittel touched the head seemed to happen somewhere deep inside their own heads, but it seemed like other things happening round them. It was as if the light altered, as if it became dimmer, as if a dark mist were starting to blow in front of their eyes; it was as if a low moaning wind got up somewhere far away in some hidden corner of some hidden passageway, and were rising and rumbling down the great spiral corridor towards them; as if the rocky walls were suddenly coming alive. And it was as if a hideous, buzzing voice were speaking right next to their ears, "Beware – beware – beware – beware – beware."

It was that voice above all which made Ormand cower down and cover his ears. There was something about its menace so powerful, so crushing, it almost made his heart stop beating.

Kittel, too, seemed paralysed, her fingers still resting on the smooth, cold hair of the head. Everything else in the room had faded almost to nothing; Ormand was nothing more than a twisted hump of rock on the floor. The dark mist seemed to be growing round her eyes, and she thought with horror that she must be going blind. But if anyone there had been capable of watching her, what they would have seen was her vacant, faraway look fading. The horror was somehow settling out all the confused crowd of faces and chattering voices in her mind – bringing her swiftly back to herself. Without looking at the head, she was tugging, tugging, trying to free her fingers from the cold thing they seemed to be stuck against.

Out in the passageway, Lissie saw the walls and ceiling and floor begin to heave and writhe as if they were all made of glistening skin, while Herold was clinging to her head so tightly it felt as though his claws would dig right into her skull.

Ten seconds – ten minutes, ten hours it seemed like – they remained; all the while Kittel more and more desperately tried to force her fingers away from the head. The nonsense about her dad had faded – of course she wasn't back at home! All she wanted now – all she had ever wanted in her life, it seemed – was to get her hand away from the cold, dead thing under her fingers, and go free, to scream, to panic, anything as long as it would stop the buzzing voice and the moaning wind and the dark mist . . .

And suddenly her hand was her own again. They were free! Kittel heard the boy across the chamber give a groan, and saw him start to crawl towards the doorway. The dark mist was clearing a little. The voice was still there, the wind, the writhing of the walls, but it wasn't as bad as it had been; it didn't make you unable to move, it left you free at least to –

To run! One by one, Lissie, Ormand and Kittel began to stumble blindly, faster and faster, half in terror of some following evil, half in relief at getting away from the awful whatever-it-was that had seized on them in the central chamber. On and on, down the writhing, mist-darkened, moaning corridors, on and on, faster and faster along the way they had so uncertainly come, through the widening coils, on and on, on and on . . .

Until, surely, they were in the outer circle, stumbling past the now red-sputtering torches, Lissie still in the lead, Herold flapping along grimly beside her, Ormand following, Kittel, her breath coming in painful gasps, bringing up the rear.

They were near the outside, but how were they going to get out? Lissie remembered the door, but she also remembered the blank wall where the door had been; Kittel could remember nothing – nothing but standing on the lake shore with Herold while the soft mist writhed towards them out of the trees... Must they stumble on, round and round this awful outer corridor, until one by one they ran into the blank end wall and had to turn?

With a downward explosion of earth and stones, then a downward explosion of light – the common, blinding light of everyday – the ceiling of the passage a short distance ahead of them was torn open. They came to an abrupt halt, Ormand running slam into Lissie, Kittel tripping crack over Ormand's heel and finishing up on her hands and knees. Herold flew on and seemed to have disappeared in the cloud of settling dust. They had come to the end of their running; but were they free? Was it as easy as that?

Something was moving in the hole that had appeared in the ceiling. Something small, black, wedge-shaped, waving to and fro. The thing disappeared from the bright hole, but a second later reappeared hanging from the ceiling of the tunnel, still keeping up its sinister waving to and fro, extending steadily downwards. Lissie gave a little gasp and shrank back against Ormand, who stepped back on to Kittel's leg and nearly lost his balance. Sliding down into the tunnel from above was coil after coil of black and red snake.

From the ceiling down to the pile of stones

and earth on the floor the snake stretched, and when its throat had reached the ground, the remainder of its length slithered down after it. But none of the three children in the tunnel could move, not even Kittel who, still on her hands and knees, was looking more or less straight into the snake's pale, expressionless eyes. Something about those eyes held them absolutely still. They had run to the end of their running; all they could do now was wait for whatever would happen to them.

12

THE VAULT OF THE BEAR

"What about that rope?" a clear, piping voice said.

Bull jumped, clean off the ground, for he had thought he was alone. He looked round, but it was several moments before he saw the speaker, sitting in a tree just above his head. It was a white-haired, wrinkle-faced, green-eyed, green-coated old man, and he was so small he could almost have sat in the palm of Bull's hand.

"Who on earth are you?" Bull exclaimed. "Are you – you're not Puckel, are you?"

"Sparrow sent me," the tiny man piped. "I am his messenger."

"He never said he'd be sending a messenger," said Bull cautiously.

"He never said he wouldn't," the reply came. "But if you don't want a messenger, then I'm not his messenger, and be blowed to his message. I'm off." And he leaped to his feet and walked down to the end of his gently swaying branch.

"Wait," said Bull. "I didn't want – I didn't mean to make you angry. It's just – there's a lot of queer things going on. I don't know who I can trust."

The little man put his hands behind his back and pirouetted a couple of times on a twig, looking down at his feet.

"I'm sorry," said Bull. Bull didn't often say sorry to anyone, and the word only came out with a great effort. It was hard to say if the stranger appreciated the effort; he just went on looking down at his feet.

But presently he said, "Anyway, I gave it you."

"Did you?" said Bull. "What did you say?"

"I never repeat myself."

"Then what's the point – " Bull began, and checked himself, at the same time remembering the little man had said something about –

"What rope do you mean?" Bull enquired.

"Aha, so you heard me!" the piping voice said.

"I remember now."

"What else do you remember?"

"Well – there was a rope Sparrow used, way back when... I don't think anyone saw it often. It was Puckel's rope, I know that. It can't still be in Gogs' house, can it? That's

155

when I last saw it . . ."

The little man jumped from the branch-end to the ground, trailing an arc of green light behind him. He stood in front of Bull, his head no higher than Bull's knee. "A rope to bind the fallen people," he said. "The dead not dead. Those you trust to go armed, day and night – crossed wood, shaft wood. Those you trust to pin down the tricksters with wood and iron. Then trussed in the rope where they fall."

"Did Sparrow tell you to say all that as well?" Bull asked in some surprise.

"Every word," the little man piped, and melted away into the grass.

Bull blinked, scratched his head. He felt a little shaken, and didn't much like the idea of being watched without his knowing. Where was Sparrow anyway? Had Cross Lurgan and Noddy Borrow found him? And was that Puckel he had just seen? Apart from the size, he looked just like Sparrow's description of the old man of the mountains.

Sparrow said, "Can I see Bull because of the Secret Way?"

"No, clod-head," the stick replied. "You can see him because of me. Your messenger reached him by the Secret Way. I am letting you see this so that you will see how the Way can be used."

Sparrow chuckled, despite his aching head

and his throbbing, blinded eye. He had found the little Puckel-messenger very droll. "He shouldn't have said I told him to say all that, though," he said. "That wasn't true."

"When you don't even know who you are, how can you say what messages you may or may not have given?" said the stick.

Sparrow was silent, gazing painfully into the pool of water the snake had led him to in the dark, before it had turned back into the stick again. He could see nothing of where the pool was or what kind of place they were in. All that was to be seen was the still surface of the water and in its depths the small figure of Bull, who was now toiling up the hill towards Gogs' house. Sparrow saw him slipping in through the front door without knocking. The house seemed to be deserted, though he saw Gogs' father working with a hoe in the field at the back.

The picture in the pool was changing constantly, showing Sparrow now a wide stretch of field and wood and hillside, now things very close up. He could see Bull in the little downstairs bedroom, scrabbling under the bed, pulling out old boots, an old pan lid, dust and cobwebs and, finally, something that looked like the biggest cobweb of all, but which Bull shook, then wound up and slung over his shoulder: a thin grey rope, the very one Sparrow and Kittel had brought down from Puckel's cave eighteen months before. It wasn't surprising it had been overlooked for so long; when Sparrow and Kittel had used it before, it had been invisible to most people.

The surface of the pool rippled and the scene changed completely. There was a crowd of people in a large hall — the village hall, Sparrow realized, and Ms Redwall was up on a platform making an impassioned speech. Everything seemed confused.

"To sweep out the dirt from under our beds," he heard Ms Redwall declaiming, "to bring back a sense of independence to his village, a pride in ourselves and what we can achieve without the help of any outsiders..." There was a lot more which Sparrow found hard to understand. A tremendous number of people seemed to be there, outside in the square as well as in the hall itself. Gradually, from things he could understand, he realized that Ms Redwall was talking about the Traders, and urging the village people to ban them all from the village for ever. She kept reminding them of Lissie's mother, "her mind quite destroyed", and saying that she had gone mad because of the strain of being married to a Trader, and that that was what would happen to the whole village if the Traders didn't go.

Sparrow felt a cold lump of fear growing in his stomach. What had been going on since he left? Had everything gone quite crazy? He remembered Gogs' deserted house – but then, there was Gogs' father out in the field. No, not everyone would be at this meeting. Some people, surely, wouldn't listen to this awful woman.

Almost immediately the scene changed again. He could still hear Ms Redwall's voice ranting away somewhere in the distance, but what he saw now was a small room full of people, men and women standing silently, listening to the distant voice with despairing faces. Plato Smithers was among them.

The picture in the pool faded. As it disappeared, Sparrow saw Bull come into the room and start to tell the people that he had had a message from Sparrow and that they were to have their crossbows with them at all times.

The water in the pool didn't go completely dark, and presently Sparrow realized that this was because he now had some idea of their surroundings. He seemed to be standing on the ground under a dark, starless sky. The eye where the snake struck him throbbed and seemed to be completely blind – but it was real darkness which was stopping him seeing properly. Dimly his good eye made out the dark massed shape of five huge trees surrounding a pool. They were holly trees, the biggest he had ever seen. "This must be Lissie's pool," he murmured. "Where she went. At Villas."

"It is called the Hollywell," the stick said. "It is most often the centre of the Enclosure. Does your eye pain you?"

"Yes," Sparrow said.

"It will heal. When the time comes, it will be your eyes which tell you the truth. One eye to see the dreaming, one to see through it. We are at the Centre. From here all the angles of the Giants' Door can be seen. Look into the water."

Sparrow looked. At first he thought there was going to be another picture, but gradually it seemed rather that there was something like a disc of pure, shining blue lying at the bottom of the pool. Then he realized that the sand and gravel at the bottom had actually become transparent and the blue disc was beneath.

"Because you will see through all illusion, you will have no more need of your stone. Throw it into the pool."

"Why?" Sparrow exclaimed.

"Do as you're told." The stick was wrapped round his arm again, and now he thought he felt its grip tightening.

Reluctantly he drew the little rough pyramid out of his pouch and weighed it in his hand.

"It was supposed to go back and become a mountain again," he said. "I'm supposed to give it back to Puckel."

"What you are supposed to do with it, young slug, is what I tell you to do with it," the stick returned. "Now will you throw it, or will I have to twist your arm off first?"

There was no doubt of it – the stick was squeezing Sparrow's arm tighter and tighter. After what it had done to his eye, he thought it would have little difficulty in ridding him of an arm as well. "What'll happen to the stone?" he asked.

"Obviously, it will become a mountain," the stick replied drily. And Sparrow felt the pressure on his arm slackening. He took a deep breath and gently threw the stone towards the pool. It was like throwing a part of himself away.

There was barely a ripple. Sparrow watched, fascinated, as the stone seemed to float gently downwards – as if through thick oil – and then on, down, through the bottom, as if the gravel and sand were nothing but shadows across the blue disc. Suddenly the stone grew rapidly smaller. Sparrow bent forwards to see. It took him a moment to realize that it was not getting smaller but was falling, falling away through a great sky of pure, cloudless blue, falling into some measureless abyss of air. That was what the disc was! Not a disc at

161

all, but a doorway through into some other place. Sparrow gazed and gazed, although by now the stone had fallen far out of sight. Try as he might, he could see no ground, no far-distant hazy earth for the stone to fall to . . .

Gradually the bright blue of that other-worldly sky changed to dark blue, and from dark blue to black: and the blackness rose up out of the hole in the bottom of the pool and gathered itself round Sparrow. All sight faded, all sense, all sound. Feeling vaguely for his arm, Sparrow noticed that the stick was gone; he was alone. His heart beat fast, then slowed. Time might have passed, there in the sightless dark, but even his heartbeat had grown so quiet and slow that there was nothing by which to measure it.

"We must wait for the moon to rise," said a dry, scrapy voice beside his ear.

Sparrow started, and his heart was beating again. It was the stick's voice, but not quite the stick's voice . . . It seemed to have grown gentler; in fact, it reminded Sparrow strongly of his old teacher, Ms Minn.

"Be calm," the voice said. "This is a strange place, because it is not really any place but the end of all places. In the daylight world it can't be found; but here, in the darkness, all things come together. This is the Enclosure. Listen now, and I shall tell you the names of the five angles, and when I finish, the moon will rise.

"The Star Wheel you know of from my brother. The Vault of the Bear you will come to shortly. These make up one side of the Door. Remember the names; one day you will need to know them. Facing these two are the Scroll Cupboard and Mother Egg; and at the top King Puck, which holds the whole doorway together."

And the moon was there. There had been no rising, no slow gathering of light on a dark horizon; simply, one moment complete blackness, the next, the calm, milky moon. Sparrow was standing in a circle of high, steep rocks, and before him there was a cave.

It was not the only cave in that dark, rocky enclosure. He turned a little to the left, and saw another. He turned again; his eyes picked out a third in the deep shadow cast by the moon.

There were five caves altogether, spaced regularly round the rocky walls. Five black, secret mouths in a circle round him; and he was alone in the circle in the moonlight; the stick was gone from his arm; the snake was not there.

He gazed up at the blue-creamy orb in the black sky. A wisp of cloud moved across it, like a tangle of hair over a wild old, mild old face. Sparrow asked the moon. "Why did I need to hear the names?"

The moon replied, in the voice that was like

the stick's voice but not quite the stick's voice. "Understand," it said, "that you do both the things you want to do and the things which must be done. So, there is a way home for the girl, and you will find it. You have been told this already. Why do you imagine you were given magical gifts?"

"To help her get back home?" Sparrow suggested.

"You say to help her get back home," the moon said. "But this is only what you *want* to do. There is also the thing which *must be done*. The way which you and the girl will find is this thing. You will not find it only for her or for yourself, but for many others. The girl was brought here so that she and you should find the way back. Now, I ask again – why do you imagine you were given magical gifts?"

"Well," Sparrow answered uncertainly, "I helped Puckel when he had fallen down through—"

"You are wrong again," the moon interrupted. "Your gifts were to prepare you for learning the Secret Way of the Mountains. Games to play, but games with a purpose. The learning of the Secret Way also has a purpose, but mastering the masters of the dreaming is no game. It is part of a battle with deadly danger. You were needed for this and chosen for this, and soon you will face the hardest test of all, which will decide whether the choice was a right one."

"What's that?" Sparrow breathed, now thoroughly alarmed.

"If I told you anything about it, it might ruin your chance of coming through," the moon replied. "Puckel believes you will pass the test; he believes you are your father's son."

"What's my father got to do with it?"

"Everything," the moon replied.

There was a silence. For a while Sparrow felt too confused to speak. Then all his doubts and confusion came together in a single question, the question he had been longing for years to ask of someone who might know the answer. And here was someone – or something – who seemed to know. "What happened to my father?" he asked.

"He was eaten by a bear." The moon floated in the black sky, expressionless.

"Oh," said Sparrow. He felt cold.

"Now you must do what you're here to do," said the moon. "The cave you are looking at leads to the Vault of the Bear. You remember your task?"

"I've to try and find out what the Polymorphs have stolen from it."

"Do it then."

Sparrow walked over the uneven ground and entered the cave. Although the rocky mouth was in deep shadow, it was less dark inside than he had expected – or at least he could see more clearly than he had expected to. Ahead of him was a heavy wooden door with a large something carved on it where you would expect the knocker to be. Sparrow stared in the deep darkness at the carved shape. It showed a snarling bear's head – not life-sized, but very realistic. There was a wooden bar across the door. He lifted it and pushed.

He was in a small, round chamber – if he had known, very like the chamber which Kittel, Lissie and Ormand had come to in the centre of the Labyrinth. There was a shaft of moonlight slanting across from somewhere high up in the vaulted roof. It fell across a great shape on a stone couch in the centre of the chamber. With his skin crawling, Sparrow went hesitantly over to it.

It seemed to be the statue of a man lying on his back. A stone sword lay at one side of him; at his other side, cupped in his stone hand, was a stone bear's head with snarling jaws. What looked like a huge round plate lay against his feet. "A shield," Sparrow breathed. The man's clothing seemed curiously smooth in some parts – over the chest, for example – and curiosly sharp in others. "He's wearing armour," Sparrow whispered. "It's the statue of a knight, like in the stories. And the bear's head is his hood – he's the one who came to help the Traders."

Down one side of the couch Sparrow crept, round the foot, and along the other side. The shaft of moonlight fell full on the great round shield, leaving the shoulders of the statue in deep shadow. Sparrow inched softly towards the shadowed head.

The head was missing. Sparrow had to feel with his hands to be quite sure, because it was so dark at this end. But there was no doubt about it. There was a stone pillow where the head should have rested; but moving his fingers gently along the armour-plated shoulders, Sparrow could feel the stump of the neck ending in a rim of jagged stone. Some enormously powerful hands must have seized the head and broken it off.

So that was it! Sparrow wanted to make sure, and crawled about the dark floor of the chamber, searching to see if the head could simply have fallen off. But he was already certain. *This is the moving of a stone from where it should be to where it shouldn't be* – the otter's message drifted into his memory. A stone *head!*

At last he got up, went back through the door and let the bar fall into place behind him.

Out in the courtyard of rocks the milky moon gazed down.

"Was anything missing?" the moon asked.

"The head," replied Sparrow. "They've stolen the knight's head."

167

"Then we must find it. The cave next to it on your left leads to the Star Wheel; I shall go first."

Sparrow went to the next cave mouth and waited. Nothing happened.

"Come on, we haven't all night," the moon's voice came, but with just a trace of snappishness that reminded Sparrow strongly of the stick.

Still he could see no one, but he did notice that a thin moonbeam had cleared the edge of the cave mouth and was shining into the depths. Sparrow went in. And the strange thing was that, although he should have blocked off the light, the moonbeam shone as steadily as ever.

The cave was nothing like the Vault of the Bear: it was little more than a rough hollow scooped out of the rock. Sparrow turned round, bewildered. Then he noticed the floor. The floor was not rough, but polished like marble. And on it was graven a pattern of five sides. "It's the shape of the door," Sparrow said — "at the cottage and in the tower."

"You will see doors where there are doors to see," the moon — or the stick — said. "This is your door."

"Will you come with me?" asked Sparrow.

"That will depend on you. If your door is big enough, you will be able to take others with you."

Sparrow considered. "The only thing," he

168

said, "is that it isn't really a door, is it? How am I to open it?"

"Stamp on the floor," the voice whispered.

And Sparrow stamped. Once he stamped, and the floor gave back a dull, solid sound. Twice he stamped, and the floor sounded with a distant echo. Three times he stamped, and there was a noise like thunder in the walls of the cave – and suddenly everything collapsed; walls, roof, rock floor, black sky and moon disappeared and he was standing in the glaring daylight, with a summer sunrise just appearing over the edge of a hill behind him – exactly where the moon had been.

But in the grass at his feet was a great, gaping hole, through which the light fell on a pile of earth and rocks in a reddish-hued passageway. Carefully he let himself down through the hole.

13

BROKEN STONE

It took Sparrow some minutes to realize that the place Puckel and the stick called the Star Wheel must be the same as the Labyrinth of the Polymorphs. He had not been expecting to find Kittel. Even if he had been, he would certainly not have expected to so soon; he had imagined a labyrinth to be a place like the copper mine outside the village, full of complicated underground passages where you could get lost for ever. He gaped rather stupidly at the three of them before he understood, though even then he could not think how Lissie and the stranger – Ormand – had got there.

As for Kittel, Lissie and Ormand, they were so intent on the approaching snake that for a while they did not even notice the darkening of the light through the hole in the tunnel ceiling. Nor did they notice the pair of legs dangling through the hole, then the body suspended on its elbows from the top of the hole. Closer the snake slid; and it was not until it had cast its long, patterned body on the floor all about the group of children and gripped on its tail with its hard black lips that they were able to look up suddenly and see Sparrow coming towards them with – quite how, they couldn't imagine – Herold perched companionably on his shoulder.

He looked a bit breathless and a bit tousled – just like the Sparrow Lissie and Kittel knew – but even in that first moment of seeing him, the two girls immediately sensed there was something different. For a moment, it did cross Kittel's mind that this was not the real Sparrow at all, but another trick of the Polymorphs; she had after all been mistaken about her own sister. On the other hand, if this was a trick, surely they would have taken the trouble to make the trick Sparrow exactly as she remembered the real one – and this Sparrow had the most splendid black eye she had ever seen. No, it was certainly Sparrow; but something had happened to him – apart from the black eye. He was changed.

"That's the way out, I think," he said at length, pointing to the hole in the ceiling. "I don't know exactly where it goes to. But I think there may be something here I've got to collect before we can get away."

"Collect?" echoed Kittel, although she had already guessed. "What?"

"A head," Sparrow replied. "Have you seen one?"

"No!" Lissie brought out in a half scream before anyone could answer.

"Yes, we have," said Ormand, as bravely as he could, though his teeth were chattering; "but I don't think you can just collect it."

"Where is it?" Sparrow asked.

"Oh, it's easy enough to find," Lissie put in again, in a high, wavery voice. "You just follow the passage, and you're bound to come to it."

"Isn't this a labyrinth, then?" Sparrow asked.

"It's a spiral," Lissie said.

Sparrow hesitated. He could see from their faces that Kittel, Lissie and Ormand had had a severe fright. Would he be able to seize the stone head? Certainly he would have a good chance of it if he took the stick; but the stick, in its snake form, had circled itself round the three of them. It was quite obvious it intended to protect them, and not to go anywhere with Sparrow. He would have to do without.

"Is the head guarded?" he asked.

"Well, not exactly," Kittel replied uncertainly. "Not exactly guarded."

"Then what's so bad about it?" Sparrow asked. "It's just a stone head."

"Stone?" Lissie let out in a squeak of

disbelief. "You call that stone?" She was shuddering.

"What was wrong with it?" said Sparrow.

"It was alive," said Kittel after a short silence.

"Alive?" Sparrow repeated. "How?"

"I don't know," Kittel said in a low voice. "It was just a head, on a spike sort of thing, and it was speaking. It spoke to us. I can't remember much about it; I came over a bit strange. I think it must have been the head of the Polymorphs."

"No," said Sparrow in a puzzled voice. "No, it can't have been. It doesn't belong here. It's just something they've stolen. But it's only stone."

"Well, this one certainly wasn't," Kittel insisted.

Sparrow was puzzled. He had not been expecting this.

Then at last it occurred to him. Of course! Why hadn't he thought of the most obvious thing first! "You were being tricked," he explained. "It wasn't really alive at all. The Polymorphs were just making it seem alive!"

Kittel looked doubtful. Lissie and Ormand looked blank.

"I'll be back soon," Sparrow said. "You'd better not try to step over the snake. She's protecting you."

"Some protection," muttered Lissie, looking

down distastefully at the lithe, glistening creature.

Sparrow had already disappeared. Herold, overjoyed at having his old friend back, had demanded that Sparrow change into his shape there and then, and crow-shape seemed as good a way of getting along as any. So Sparrow ventured into the very heart of the Polymorphs' power without stick, stone, or even the security of being in his own body.

Before long he had drawn into the tight centre of the Star Wheel, and the murmuring voice came to his ears.

He took on his own shape again. Surprisingly, Herold didn't protest; nor did he choose to perch on Sparrow's shoulder, but fluttered down to the floor and walked like a dog at his heel as he crept towards the low voice from the central chamber. It never occurred to Sparrow that the bird was behaving in this odd fashion because it had begun to feel faint. He reached the doorway, and paused.

Slowly the hair on the back of his head began to rise. Was this an illusion? He had come looking for a stone head; without his own stone how could he tell if this talking head were real or a trick? Had he come, here in the heart of the Polymorphs' power, upon the first and strongest of the Polymorphs, Bur of the Lamps? Could he be hopelessly trapped in illusion?

Sparrow stepped backwards out of the chamber and out of sight of the head. Nothing changed, nothing stirred the smooth stream of sound, nothing stopped him from going as he had come.

Finally he went into the chamber again and spoke to the head. There seemed to be nothing else he could do; it was not a stone head, but it was the only head he had come across. "Are you the head of the statue in the Vault of the Bear?" he asked.

The torch in the chamber sent up a spout of flame, blue-edged with sparks, and then died down again; but the head didn't react. "Nongonothara rambara faiallafala," it chanted peacefully.

Suddenly, at Sparrow's feet, Herold flapped, left the ground, and with four or five feeble wing-beats flew up to the little stone table in the centre of the room, where he promptly collapsed.

"Herold, what is it?" said Sparrow, going anxiously over to the table.

Herold made no reply. The lids slowly closed over his eyes. His wings were flopped out to either side of him.

"Herold!" Sparrow said again. He did not notice that his voice was the only sound in the chamber. The head had fallen silent.

Then Herold's beak moved. "Sparrow," said a deep voice.

Sparrow looked all round – at the head, at the door, under the table. But he knew the voice had come out of Herold's beak, and it was not Herold speaking. Was it the power of the Polymorphs? In that moment, and against all common sense, Sparrow made a bold guess that it was not. There was something here, something less strong than magic, but older, deeper rooted, more homely – something he could not quite put his finger on... "How do you know my name?" he mumbled, looking now not at the crow but straight at the head.

The head only smiled, a slow, dreamy, mysterious smile. A smile, somehow, of great fondness. It was almost as though the head had known – and loved – Sparrow for years and years.

But even now, despite all the little hints and glimpses he had been given, Sparrow did not guess. A dozen questions were whirling through his mind that weren't the real question, a dozen confusions that made him unable to see what was obvious.

"Why do you have to talk through the crow?" he asked. "Why do you just talk nonsense when you're by yourself?"

Again came the head's mysterious smile. "It's not nonsense," the voice answered. "When I speak without a living mouth to speak through, what I say is not words, but the thing that words come from, little islands in the ocean

176

of sound. Before the Polymorphs parted head and body, I could speak. Now, without a living mouth to speak through, I can only sing the beginnings of words."

"Is your mouth not a living mouth?" Sparrow said. "You can smile, and you can make sounds, so you must be alive. You can't be – dead, can you?"

"I am neither one thing nor the other," the voice replied. "Don't be frightened."

"I – I don't think I am, really," said Sparrow.

"Good," the voice replied. "Then listen. There is a place where the living and the dead come together. That's all I can tell you. That place is called the Vault of the Bear. I am not dead; but I am also not alive in the way you are. I have been eaten."

"By a bear?" Sparrow said, in so soft a whisper he could hardly hear it himself.

"That's what we say," the voice of the man replied. "There is a power we call the Great Bear, whose image you see circling in the stars about the Pole Tower. This power is enclosed in the Vault of the Bear. So we say I have been eaten by the Great Bear, and my place is in its belly."

"Do you mean," Sparrow said at last in a small, rough-throated whisper, "you are – the stone man is . . ."

"Your father, Sparrow. I'm sorry we must

meet like this. The Polymorphs have prevented our meeting where we should have met, in the Vault of the Bear itself, where you could have sat by my side, and we could have talked, and from where we could have gone out together to clean the Star Wheel of the murk which was gathering in its coils. That can't happen now."

"But – but, I don't understand," Sparrow faltered. "When I was there, there was a statue, just a statue made of stone . . ."

The head smiled again. "At times, yes. Though we could still have spoken. That statue was far older than I, and was only inhabited by me after I was eaten, and before me by the father of your mother. But at times the sleep of stone would fall off me, and then my flesh would become as warm and living as when I was alive; the breastplate of my copper armour would shine in the sun. Not now. Not now that the Polymorphs have stolen the sleeping head from the sleeping body. That will never happen again."

"I've been sent here to bring you back," Sparrow said. "Puckel sent me."

"Puckel sent you," Sparrow's father agreed, "but he didn't send you to bring me back. That can never happen now. He sent you to find me."

"Well, it's the same thing, isn't it?" said Sparrow, while a cold dread crept into him.

"No," his father's voice answered. "Listen.

This head contains my power, the power Puckel gave me when I became the Guardian of the Vault of the Bear. Now the power is stolen; but the head is only the vessel the power is held in; it's no more than a bottle, a jug, a bucket. They have the power. You could pick up the head and carry it out of the Star Wheel now, and the Polymorphs wouldn't try to stop you. They wouldn't need to. It would all be illusion. As soon as your back was turned, the head would again be here in the inner chamber. Only dragon fire can now return the power to the place where it should be."

"Then what can I do?" said Sparrow despairingly.

"There is only one thing you can do," the voice replied softly. "You must destroy the vessel."

"What do you mean?" Sparrow gasped.

"The head," the deep voice replied. "You must break the head in pieces."

"No!" Sparrow wailed. He had known, deep inside himself, that this was what was coming, that this was what he feared.

"Two things the Polymorphs did not reckon on," the voice said. "One was this peculiar crow's hunger for sleep. The other was that through the sleeping crow I would be able to speak and so tell you what must be done with the head. Don't waste our chance."

"No," Sparrow said. "I can't destroy it. I can't

do that! Never! You're my father! I've always wanted to find you! I can't, I can't!"

"I'm not your father, Sparrow," the voice said when he had become silent. "Think – your father isn't a head on a steel spike! When I was your father I was a man, a whole, living man. When I took my place in the belly of the Great Bear I remained your father, and I remain your father still. We can speak to each other, but we can't do the things that fathers and sons do together. That is something you will never have. But I haven't told you to destroy *me* – only the head which the Polymorphs are using for twisted purposes."

Sparrow was shaking all over. He heard what the voice was telling him, but he couldn't understand it. "No," he said. "No, I'm not going to do it; you can't make me do that – Puckel can't make me – no one can make me. I won't – I just won't!"

And without waiting for his father to reply, Sparrow reached over, seized the head – cold as it was, and heavy, but not quite stone-like – and wrenched it off the tripod. An instant later, he was skimming along the corridor with it held firmly between his hands.

Sparrow had silenced his father – and he had never felt more miserable. He knew he had done something terribly wrong. Because he had not wanted to hear what his father was telling him, he had deliberately left the crow behind, possibly unconscious, entirely at the mercy of the Polymorphs. He knew that was an unforgivable thing to do but it had not stopped him doing it. The one thought that was filling his head was that he had found his father, and he wasn't going to give him up. He didn't concern himself about the fact that a mere head – particularly one that can't even speak – is little use to anyone; somehow, some time, he would get that sorted out. Perhaps Puckel would help, or if not Puckel, perhaps the stick – or even one of the Polymorphs. What did it matter?

It seemed like no time at all before he was rounding the steady curve of the outer circle of the Star Wheel and seeing the light ahead from the hole in the ceiling. Kittel, Lissie and Ormand were running towards him. "Quick, Sparrow, be quick!" Kittel was calling. "Something's started to happen!"

Wondering vaguely what had happened to the snake, Sparrow landed at a run and stopped in front of his friends, staring at them with a wild, confused expression but saying nothing. All three of them were talking very fast and excitedly to him, but all Sparrow could make out was something about a wind rising. It seemed they had not noticed he was holding the head. Then they did, and one by one they fell silent.

Kittel looked awed, and Ormand looked scared. But Lissie screwed her eyes tight shut, clapped her hands over her ears, and started screaming.

"I won't go with you! I won't look at that thing!" they made out among the screams. "I'll stay here in the dark and never see anyone again! Get it out of my sight! Get it out, get it out!"

"Come on," said Sparrow after a moment, "we've got to get going. Help her, you two, and follow me."

"Listen to that wind!" Ormand groaned between chattering teeth.

But Sparrow could hear no wind; he could hear nothing but the blood beating in his ears. Without looking round to check whether Ormand and Kittel had managed to get Lissie to her feet, he took a tighter grip of the head and went towards the square of light in the ceiling of the passage.

He had just set his foot on the pile of earth and stones underneath the hole when a distant squawk of rage cut through the rushing in his ears. He paused, guilt and misery forcing him to stop and think what he was doing.

"Treacherous! Traitor! Disloyal! Unworthy!" the voice screamed at him, echoing down the passageway. Kittel, Ormand and Lissie paused too and turned to see where the din was coming from. They couldn't hear the words as Sparrow could, but they could be in no doubt about what the noise meant. And for Sparrow, though used to the crow's abuse, every word cut like a knife. Herold flew straight towards him where he stood just below the bright daylight.

Straight towards his face. And Sparrow realized now that the strange, swimming motion of the bird's flight was caused by his good eye being full of tears. He blinked, and wondered when he had started crying. He wished he could stop. But he couldn't, and through his blurred vision he saw Herold, magnified to twice his usual size, flapping slowly – amazingly slowly – towards him.

Herold was actually heading for Sparrow at great speed. And it was really due to bad luck that he was heading for his face – although he had been beside himself with crow-ish fury, it would never have entered the bird's head actually to attack his friend. It was simply that he had suddenly become unconscious again, in mid-flight. And just at the last moment – the moment when he was filling the whole of Sparrow's blurred vision – his beak opened wide, and the deep, urgent voice of a man filled the corridor.

"Destroy the head!" it boomed. "Quick! Now! Here! Now! Destroy the head!" And

Herold came to the abrupt end of his flight.

Sparrow had seen it coming, but he seemed powerless to do anything about it. Herold was heading straight for his eyes. At the last moment, instinctively, he cried out and threw up his hands to shield his face. The head flew out of his grip, fell with a dull thud on to the pile of earth and rolled – with a crooked, swaggering roll – along the floor of the corridor towards Kittel, Lissie and Ormand. Kittel leaped over it. She thought Herold was attacking Sparrow and her main idea was to help him. Ormand hesitated as the head bowled along towards them, but swerved to avoid it at the last minute. Lissie did not notice it at all – until it came to a stop at her toes.

Lissie had been terrified, horrified, had screamed and had sobbed. Now, staring down at the thing on her foot, she found she was angry. There was no screaming from her now; only a whisper, but it was a whisper like the hiss of a snake. "No, I won't have it – I won't have it. Destroy the head? Yes, I'll destroy the head – I'll smash you, I will!" And as she said it, she glanced round for a weapon . . .

The first thing her eye fell on was not a stone or a piece of rubble fallen from the corridor roof. It was a stick lying unnoticed against the wall. A stick of smooth, polished wood, rather twisted, and not all that solid. But it was enough, and Lissie bounded over to it, kicking the head against the opposite wall as she did so.

A groan – the groan of a man – came from Herold's beak as the head hit the wall. Sparrow, who had sat down with the force of the crow's dive, heard it – but not Lissie. She was too intent on her work. *Thwack!* The stick made contact. The man's voice groaned again from the crow's beak. "Yes," she said, "that's one from me." *Thwack!* Another groan. "And that's – " *thwack!* – "for my mad – " *thwack!* – "mother; and that's for my mad – " *thwack!* – "friend." And now silence from the crow. Sparrow was up on his feet, running towards Lissie, yelling something as he ran. Lissie wasn't even aware of him; she heard nothing but the crack of her club on its target – saw nothing, because her eyes were tight shut. That stick may not have been heavy or solid, but it had cracked the head like an eggshell.

Sparrow launched himself – not at Lissie, but along the floor, right under her stick. When her next blow fell, it was across his back. But for all the notice he took of it, it might have been a feather duster. He lay on the floor, cradling the head in his arms and groaning, "Oh no – no!" For it was already too late – the head lay in two pieces – stone pieces: cold, lifeless, and rock hard; no head of a living man, but a piece of a statue. Lissie stopped flailing, opened her eyes and gaped.

The only one who remained calm in all the confusion was Kittel, who was always good in a crisis. She had heard the voice of the man, and by the time she had reached Sparrow on the pile of earth she had realized that Herold hadn't been attacking him at all, and that the head had taken over the crow again. She didn't know if this was a trick of the Polymorphs, but it didn't seem to make any difference. She knelt down and carefully lifted the limp body of the bird from where it lay half buried in a pile of small stones. Then she turned round to see what was going on. But though she saw Lissie laying into the head with her stick, and Ormand coming up behind her as if to restrain her, and Sparrow diving to shield the head – why was he trying to protect it? – there was something else that was taking up her attention.

There was something menacing, ominous, distantly disastrous about the wind which had again begun to rise and moan in the far-off corridors. Now and then it would gather itself and rise, for a moment, to a thunder that shook the walls (though not a breath could she feel), only to die away again. But all the time, in some way, Kittel felt it was coming closer.

Carefully, she replaced Herold on the ground and ran back to Lissie, Ormand and Sparrow. She recognized the stick. "Go on, Lissie," she said urgently, grabbing her friend by the shoulders and turning her to face the pile of earth and the daylight. "Get out of that hole, as quick as you can – and keep hold of that stick!" She gave Lissie a shove and turned to Ormand. "You've got to help me with him," she said, pointing to Sparrow. "We might have to use force." The broken head was unimportant to Kittel; she was more concerned with getting Sparrow to safety.

But Sparrow didn't need any persuasion. He seemed quite sensible, and when Kittel said they had to get out and not waste any more time, he scrambled to his feet, said, "Come on, then," and skimmed off after Lissie without a glance behind. Once at the hole, he gave her a helping heave up through the broken roof, then turned and helped Ormand and Kittel through as well. Kittel, who had taken charge of Herold again, thought Sparrow must suddenly be feeling better – whatever had been wrong with him – but she noticed he was as pale as putty.

Kittel scrambled up a steep bank of soft, yielding soil, and then she was lying between Ormand and Lissie on short, sweet-smelling grass. A second later Sparrow flew up through the hole in the earth and crouched beside them, looking round him. "I see," he said at last. "I see."

By now Lissie had looked up too. "Where on earth are we?" she exclaimed.

"In the Valley of Murmuring Water," Sparrow answered in a dull voice. "But we don't have a moment to lose."

14

THE RAIN BEGINS

Sparrow had had almost as much as he could take. Looking round now in the bright sunlight of the Valley of Murmuring Water, he was scarcely able to wonder that, all the while they had been living and working there, the Labyrinth of the Polymorphs had been under their very feet.

Listlessly he looked out over the bright little meadow. What was that strange movement in the grass – as if the land were bubbling? He rubbed his eyes and peered. What was he supposed to be doing?

It was Kittel who raised the alarm and got him moving. "Listen, Sparrow," she said, her voice hard with anxiety, "that's that wind we heard getting up; it's making the whole ground move. We have to get away from here."

Sparrow listened, and looked. The ground

wasn't actually bubbling; what he could see as he stared across the valley up towards the cottage and to the foot of the mountain, was the spiral shape of the Star Wheel heaving in the ground, as though an enormous coiled worm were burrowing just below the surface. It was true; something was happening, something dangerous. It was risky, Puckel had said, to open a door between a place of power and the world of everyday. Where were Gogs and Murie? Were they somewhere out here, playing the fool with the cow and the goat?

"Come on," he said, scrambling to his feet, but almost immediately collapsing again to a crouch. "We've got to get there . . ."

"Where?" asked Kittel wildly. "Where can we go?"

"The cottage," Sparrow muttered, trying to summon up the energy to get up and run.

"That's crazy," Kittel exclaimed. "That's right in the middle of it all! Just look!"

"I know," Sparrow answered, a little snappishly now because he was trying so hard to stay sensible and practical. "It's – it's an island. It's the only safe place. We've got to get everyone there."

Somehow they managed it, though the ground was difficult to walk on, and every now and again a great heave of the grass sent them staggering to their knees. All of them could hear the rising of the subterranean

190

wind, growing now and then into gusts which bellowed out of the hole in the ground like the winding of a gigantic horn.

"Here," gasped Sparrow, as they were again tumbled off their feet in front of the little house; "we're safe here. Stay where you are."

The others looked doubtful. Sparrow staggered to the door of the house and seemed half to collapse there, leaning against one of the great stone doorposts. A moment later Kittel heard him repeating Gogs' and Murie's names.

"What's wrong? Aren't they in there?" Kittel said, getting up and coming over.

"Here they are!" Lissie called to him. "They must have been round the back of the house. They're here – so's the cow and the goat!"

Sparrow was sitting in the doorway. "Give me Herold, Kittel," he said, without so much as a glance to see if Gogs and Murie were unenchanted or not.

"I've got Herold – he's quite safe," Kittel replied, gently stroking the still body of the bird.

"Give him to me," Sparrow repeated. "Just give me him, and go and make sure the others stay here – right here, close to the door."

"All right," Kittel said quietly, looking at him anxiously. She handed him the crow and turned away. Sparrow, carefully cradling Herold against his chest, crawled into the dark shadows of the cottage.

Kittel, turning back to the others, saw that Ormand and Lissie had got up and were wandering away, looking disbelievingly at the small, hidden valley in the mountains and the wild heaving of its grassy floor. "Sparrow says you mustn't go away from the house!" Kittel called to them.

Ormand immediately came back, but although Lissie didn't go any further, she didn't follow him. Kittel turned to greet Gogs and Murie, who were standing by the corner of the house, looking bewildered. Murie had been having a dream, as she thought, of being the May Queen at a most unusual village festival. But since the "dream" had lasted three days and nights, during which she had had no food, she felt very shaky. Gogs was little better off, but at least he wasn't suffering from a badly-bruised rump.

Lissie was still holding the stick as she watched the turmoil of the valley floor, and the moment Kittel called, she felt it jerk in her hand, and heard a quiet, but sharp and not very friendly voice say, "Throw me into the air."

Lissie looked round. She couldn't see where the voice had come from. The stick jerked again, very sharply. "Me – me – me, noddle-head; throw me into the air."

It was unmistakable. The voice was coming from the stick. As it spoke, it jerked. Lissie gazed down at it in astonishment. Her hand relaxed, and she let go.

The stick didn't fall. It remained suspended above the ground, just where she had been holding it. Then it jerked again, and seemed to move menacingly towards Lissie.

"Will you throw me into the air – or will I have to knock some sense into you first?" it grated.

"No – I mean, yes," Lissie said hurriedly.

"Then do it – now."

Lissie gulped and took hold of the stick again. "Where will I throw you?"

"Into the sun, of course," the stick retorted. "Then shout like mad when the rain begins. *Remind* Sparrow, since he seems to have lost his wits. Now, whirl me round, and throw, as hard as you can. It's a long way up to the sun."

"Yes, it is," agreed Lissie, and started to whirl the stick, too frightened to disobey.

Whizz – whizz – whizz! Lissie whirled the stick round above her head. A wind – a wind in the air, not at all like the bellowing gale under the ground – seemed to gather around it.

"Lissie – what are you doing?" She dimly heard Kittel's warning yell.

"Now!" cracked the stick's voice; and Lissie let go.

"Lissie!" came Kittel's scream.

But Lissie couldn't have disobeyed the stick, even if she had wanted to. It left her hand and shot up into the air straight for the sun, which by now was standing high above the wood beyond the stream. Quickly, Lissie turned and scampered back to give her message to Sparrow in the cottage.

She sped to the door, then stopped. Sparrow was there, but he was far away, unaware of anything that was going on. And despite the din of the seething earth and the bellowing horn of the underground wind, in the cottage there was absolute silence, and in the silence there was the distinct sound of a man's voice, softly – painfully – speaking. Lissie looked round doubtfully – and that was the moment when the earth burst open, and with a hissing roar like steam escaping from a steam-boiler the keepers of the Labyrinth came into the open. Lissie forgot everything else.

Sparrow heard none of it. In the darkness of the cottage he seemed to be enclosed in a shell, like a chicken waiting to be hatched. The man's voice had spoken from the crow's beak almost as soon as he had stumbled through the door, and though it was quiet, scarcely above a whisper, Sparrow had no difficulty in hearing it in the absolute stillness of the four walls.

"Sparrow," the voice said.

"Father?" said Sparrow in a small, wondering voice. "Are you still here?"

"I'm still here," the voice returned. "But

not for long. Your friend is dying, and in a moment I must leave you alone with him. You shouldn't part with him while he feels you betrayed him."

"I'm going to lose Herold too," Sparrow blurted out in a sob. "I'm going to lose everything. Kittel's going to go as well – I don't know when but I know she will, and I'm going to be left alone and Puckel and – and . . ."

"Hush," his father's voice whispered. "It won't be as bad as that, you'll see. Things are a lot better than you think. The head was destroyed, in the Star Wheel too – just as it should have been. The Polymorphs are in great trouble."

"Yes," Sparrow answered drearily, "but if your head's been destroyed, you won't be here any longer, will you? And if Herold's dying . . . Father, where will you be? You'll be gone, you'll have disappeared – it'll all be like it was before I found you, before—"

"Well, it was all right then, wasn't it?" his father interrupted him. "You managed, didn't you?"

"Yes, but that was before . . ." there seemed to be a knot in Sparrow's chest, and he was finding it difficult to speak. "It would have been better if everything had just stayed like that – if I'd never found you at all." He was clutching the body of Herold close against his stomach, cradling it passionately, full of the terrible fear of loss.

"Come," the man's voice whispered back at him out of the crow's beak. "You'd be quite surprised where I can get to. That otter, for example..."

"What about it?" Sparrow's interest kindled, in spite of himself.

The voice chuckled. "Otters are clever beasts, but they're not *that* clever. That was your old dad, letting you know he was in trouble."

"What? How?" Sparrow stammered.

"There's not much time," Sparrow's father answered, "but that was when my head had been removed from the Vault of the Bear and was being taken to the Star Wheel. I could put my thought into the otter's brain, though at that stage I couldn't talk human words through its mouth. Luckily, you had been well taught, and knew what the otter was saying."

"I would never have thought of my stone — and the Pole Star — if it hadn't been for that!" Sparrow exclaimed. "And then I might never have found my way to Puckel and — what about the other time? Was that you too? But why did...?"

"That's as much time as we can have now. But we'll speak again. No — don't interrupt. You'll have work to do in a moment. The song, remember. All join hands... Goodbye for now, Sparrow. Be sure of yourself!"

"But I'm not . . . No, wait . . . Father! Don't go yet! Not yet! I want to . . ."

But he knew it was too late. The beak had closed. The black, hard eye had opened and was regarding him fixedly. Herold's chest gave a heave. Then the beak opened again, and one or two unintelligible squeaks and whiffles came out of it, as though the bird were clearing its throat. At last the voice spoke – not the man's voice any more, talking in human language, but the bird's voice, speaking the language that only Sparrow knew. "Friend . . ." it croaked. "Friend."

Sparrow couldn't bear it. "Oh, Herold," he groaned; "I left you behind – you could have been . . ."

"Nothing," the crow croaked – so softly now it was almost inaudible. "It was nothing."

"I'm sorry, Herold," Sparrow's voice sang the words softly over the top of a sob.

"Bounteous boy," the crow answered, while for a brief second his eye sparkled with its old life. He seemed to be summoning up one last great effort. "Everything I had was from you. Now the vessel is shattered, and your servant can depart in peace."

At any other time, Sparrow would have laughed over the crow's pompous words. As he looked down at the limp bundle of feathers in his hands, the crow's chest gave another great

197

heave – a long, long breath out. Then Sparrow realized that the black beady eye was no longer seeing anything. Herold was gone. Gently, he laid the body on the floor and straightened up.

Without knowing why, he suddenly felt a lot better.

Outside the cottage, Kittel, Lissie, Ormand, Murie and Gogs gaped in horrified amazement. Where the small hole in the grass had marked the outermost circle of the Star Wheel there was now a massive, brown rent. Smoke billowed round its edges, staining the grass a dirty grey. And from the hole itself there coiled and climbed a shape that was not a shape, something that was not something, that baffled the eyes and confused the senses. There seemed to be faces in it, human faces or animal faces or faces half human, half animal; big faces, little faces, ugly faces, sad or furious faces, pudgy faces, noble faces, terrifying faces, faces peeping shyly or mischievously, faces blankly staring into great distances like the faces of statues... But human or animal, bird, fish or insect, the faces all the while seemed to be trying to drag themselves away out of the Thing, but as soon as they came out of it and became almost clear they were dragged back in. And the thing went on and on, pouring out of the hole, filling the air, darkening the sun, pouring upwards endlessly, more and more and more shapes and forms and faces.

When it filled half the sky, it changed. The shapes and faces kept pouring on and upwards out of the hole, but now there were whole scenes. There was nothing pleasant – only things decaying, collapsing, crumbling. A castle of stone rose up, and almost immediately slipped and slid into the wide moat of green water surrounding it. A horse was pulling a cart – the axle cracked and the wheels fell off, and the horse collapsed into slime and bones. Dead animals and the branches of trees floated by in the flood of a great, grey swollen river.

Lissie standing next to Murie, felt for her hand and gripped it tightly. "What is it?" she whispered.

Murie shook her head. "I don't know," she whispered back.

"It's horrible," Ormand muttered.

Though spreading over the whole sky, no part of the shadow came near them as they stood at the door of the cottage. But their eyes kept returning to a sort of mass or knot of darkness which seemed to be forming low down in its skirts. "What are we supposed to do?" Kittel said.

"Shout!" Sparrow's voice answered her.

Tearing their eyes away from the pouring Thing, all five of them turned round to see Sparrow, standing in the cottage doorway.

He looked pale, his eyes were red-rimmed, his cheeks were extremely grubby, but though he gazed upwards at the tainted sky, there was a confident look on his face – almost a smile. And even as he came out from the doorway, gazing upwards, a great drop of water splashed on his nose and rolled down his cheek. Then another hit him smack in the eye and his face screwed up.

Splash! Splash! Massive drops of rain were coming down all round. Two of them were enough to make your head feel wet all over; on the roof they crashed into the warm thatch and hissed and steamed. The young plants in the garden were doing a slow-motion tango as the great gouts of water battered on their leaves. Faster the rain began to fall, but no less heavily, and all over the valley a sound like distant drumming began.

"Of course!" Lissie exclaimed. "That's what I had to tell you, Sparrow. We shout like mad when the drums – I mean the rain – begins!"

The force of the rain grew. Over the valley it no longer looked like rain, but like straight rods of grey steel, and the sound of the stream was already growing to a roar. The noise was becoming unbearable; if they looked upwards it was difficult to breathe for the crashing downpour. With an effort Lissie stared towards the sky. Still the endless procession of shapes and faces was up there, but all was coiling and writhing, and with tremendous relief she realized that the rain was not coming from the Thing spread through the sky, but from something above and beyond it. She looked down, gasping for breath.

"We've got to shout — as loud as we can!" Sparrow yelled above the tumult.

"Why?" Murie yelled back at him.

"I don't know!"

"What?"

"I don't know!"

"Oh — look!" Kittel screamed. "Look at it! Look! Look!"

The knot of darkness had formed into something like a tunnel — a dark, rocky track winding down out of a tunnel of murk; and there were two figures on the track, coming towards them, one bright, one dark, but both surrounded by an air of cruel menace.

"Oh, no," Sparrow heard Ormand whimpering, "it's him, with the lantern."

And it was about then that Sparrow discovered a difference in his eyes. The figures of the two Polymorphs became like shadows round something which he couldn't see properly — as though his eyes were tired and he were seeing double. And there was a third figure, like a shadow, huge, in front of them. What was happening? What had the stick said? One eye to see the dream.... Like the way Herold looked at you, perhaps, out of one eye and then the other. Sparrow covered his left eye – the damaged one – and the two figures became clear again, while the great shadow vanished. There, hastening on with huge jumping strides of its spidery legs, was the lantern-carrying horror which had shut Lissie and Ormand into the maze of the Polymorphs. And there beside it, flaming in gold and green light, strode the beautiful lady who had first ensnared Sparrow in the gully.

Sparrow covered his right eye, and let out a startled cry.

The blind eye could see, but not in the ordinary way; it was showing him what was behind the illusion of the Polymorphs' appearance. He had not had time to look at them clearly on the two occasions he had met them before, and there had been some things about their shape he had not understood. Now he saw the high, domed foreheads properly, the stooped shoulders that did not end in arms but in huge wings that bore the creatures clear of the ground; he saw the unearthly ugliness of them. And there were not two, but three.

The lady and the lantern carrier were advancing behind another huge form that could not be seen at all by normal vision. It was like them; had the same great shaggy wings with the same slow, sickening beat – but it had two heads, and in the centre of each head was a glaring eye. The two heads swung imperiously this way and that, like a hunting beast searching for sight of its prey. The two glaring eyes were like lamps, one of them red-gold, one so pale it was almost white...

"Bur of the Lamps — if you'd seen him, you'd have known about it..." Sparrow remembered Puckel's words. This, he had no doubt, was the head of the Polymorphs; and the three were coming straight for them, stooping out of some unguessed depth of grey sky. Illusion or no illusion, Sparrow didn't like the look of either vision of the Polymorphs, but it was the awful eyes in the wild-swinging heads of the leader that most filled him with dismay.

"Bur of the Lamps; Ur, the linden lady; Eych, the Enslaver," he said aloud.

"What?" Murie said, staring at the advancing figures.

"Their names. They're called Ur, Eych and Bur."

"Ureych?" said Murie. "What sort of name's that?"

"They've stopped," Kittel exclaimed.

They had, but it was only a pause; a moment later they were advancing again. It was hard for Sparrow to tell exactly how far away they were, but on the rocky illusion-road they seemed to be about the distance of the stream.

"That's it!" Sparrow yelled. "Their names! We shout out their names! All their names!

After me. There's more than two; just say them after me. Ur!"

The six of them clustered round. "Ur!" they shouted.

"All join hands, like in the song!" Sparrow said. "Now – Eych!"

"Eych!" they shouted, fumbling for each other's hands, but not daring to take their eyes off the approaching danger.

Feverishly, Sparrow cast back in his mind over the names he had heard from Puckel. He felt them all there in his memory, but still he worried he might forget them. Maybe the other three who weren't here didn't matter... Who were they, anyway? There was –

"Yo!" He shouted it as he remembered it.

"Yo!" the others shouted. The figures of Ur and Eych stopped and looked behind them. Did they expect their companions to be there? But twin-headed Bur advanced.

"Bur!" Sparrow screamed, and the others repeated it. The monster halted.

"Eni! and Tho!"

"Eni! Tho!" But now the three were coming forward again. From his right eye Sparrow saw they had crossed the stream and were stepping up through the mown hay.

"Ur! Eych! Yo! Bur! Eni! Tho!" Sparrow yelled, speeding the names together.

"Ur! Eych! Yo! Bur! Eni! Tho!" Their voices seemed to get caught in the rhythm of the teeming rain, the names of the Polymorphs ran together as if the rain had washed their edges away. They repeated them over and over, faster and faster – Ureychyoburenitho! Ureychyoburenitho! The three Polymorphs had halted, uncertain it seemed – or perhaps waiting...

What was Sparrow to do? They couldn't go on shouting the names forever. The Polymorphs had halted, but they didn't look as though they were going to go away...

And then the truth hit Sparrow. How he suddenly understood it he didn't know, but he was in no doubt: Ureychyoburenitho was the name of the dragon. They were standing there in a ring, calling out the dragon's name. And Puckel had said that calling out the dragon's name was the one thing that would bring it back to the earth.

15

UREYCHYOBURENITHO

In the square at Copperhill, screams and shouts filled the air. The glaring eyes of the stone rams' heads on the village hall did not glare as horribly as the eyes of the two men who stood under the linden trees, with crossbows raised. Crossbow bolts were already lodged deep in the wood of a windowsill and a door, on houses across the square. Another lay where it had sheared off the top of a stone gatepost, and one stood through Plato Smithers' felt hat. People were fleeing in all directions up the small streets that led from the square. The two men under the linden trees shouted in harsh, barking voices, but their words were gibberish. Cross Lurgan and Noddy Borrow had returned from the mountains empty-handed and stark mad.

The scattering people found shelter, and a

watching silence fell, broken only by the occasional shouts of the two men.

"Eych! Tho!" Cross Lurgan shouted.

"Ur Yo Eni Bur!" Noddy Borrow barked back.

Briefly, Plato Smithers appeared up on the balcony of the village hall, a crossbow in one hand, waving with the other over the square to where a second bowman crept stealthily behind a hedge. A third slipped gingerly from trunk to trunk of the lindens towards the tree by which Lurgan and Borrow stood.

At that moment there was a small commotion in one of the streets, and into full view of those in the square stepped the stately figure of Ms Redwall. Gasps of admiration broke from the hiding people as, without a trace of fear, she swept across the square towards the lindens.

"Boro Bur Oro Ur!" Cross Lurgan screamed.

"Ya Yo Eni Eni!" Noddy Borrow howled.

Ms Redwall's most imperious voice interrupted them. "Just put those things down, you two, and don't be so silly. We've had quite enough of this nonsense."

With more senseless yells, both madmen fired. The cruel whizz of the two bolts could be heard all over the square. Time seemed to stand still. *Thack-whoo! Thack-whoo!* echoed from the walls as Plato Smithers and his comrades fired the bolts from their own weapons. Ms Redwall crumpled and fell, a single bolt through her neck. Lurgan and Borrow, both hit, ran jerking forwards before somersaulting into a heap beside their victim.

The silence went on for a minute or more, before people started drifting slowly back into the square. Plato Smithers leaned over the balcony of the hall, white-faced and shaking in every one of his huge limbs. A wide ring collected about the three fallen villagers, as the people stared down in silent horror. Never before had such a thing happened in Copperhill.

"Mr Smithers!" a clear voice called up from below the balcony, and Smithers turned his head to find himself in the steady stare of Bull Hind's blue eyes. The big man rubbed his own eyes, and his felt hat slipped off, unbalanced by the weight of the bolt through its crown. Was that a tiny white-haired man standing by the boy's knee? Plato Smithers rubbed his eyes again and tried to concentrate. Bull was holding up a rope. "Do you see this?" he asked.

There was something flimsy, almost misty, about the rope, but it was quite visible. Smithers nodded.

"We have to tie them up in it. They aren't dead. We have to tie them up in the rope, all together. Do you understand?"

Smithers pushed himself upright and turned and staggered back through the balcony door. A few moments later he was down in the square at Bull's side, looking a bit steadier. "I don't know what all this is about, lad," he said, "but I'm going to do what you say."

Together they walked over to the silent crowd.

Sparrow couldn't help it. He had to shout, he had to call the dragon's name. And strangely, although he knew what he was doing, he found he had no fear. The very sound of the name seemed to fill him with a fierce, wild excitement, and in his mind's eye he saw the great, fiery demon-beast rushing and whirling down from a darkness behind the sun. Nearer it would be coming, nearer still . . .

Over and again they called out the strange name, none of them except Sparrow knowing what they were doing. And now the three visible Polymorphs were turning round. Round and round, slowly at first and then quickening as though in some weird bird-dance, with their wings flapping and churning about them. Ureychyoburenitho! At first Sparrow suspected a new trick – perhaps they were dancing up a storm of their own. But presently he became sure that they were whirling because they couldn't help it, just as the Traders had danced because they couldn't help it, all those years before. He laughed.

Ureychyoburenitho!

And with a roaring of the air, and a crackling

and a hissing, the dark Thing which had burst out of the ground split into a thousand pieces. Faces, figures and forms went whirling and twirling off into the sky, or were beaten down to the earth by the rain. The three Polymorphs, in their own shapes – even Bur was just visible to the others now – went on turning and turning, but they were unmistakably on the ordinary ground now, down in the hay meadow, ordinary-sized, unimpressive, ragged figures.

And the dragon came, splitting the clouds apart, while the sun burst through in dazzling rainbows and the rain turned to great cork-screw columns that seemed to dance on the ground. Downwards the massive beast whirled, bellowing like thunder, landing with an almighty crash on the ground between them and the whirling Polymorphs. The shock of its fall knocked the feet from under them and sent them sprawling in the mud. All but one of the dancing columns of water disappeared, and that one corkscrewed for a while beside the dragon as it gave a few more roars and blasts and then grew still. A small figure perched high on its back reached over and the column of water danced up into the outstretched hand, and shrank and grew dark; and there was Puckel, holding his stick again, then digging it into the dragon's side and vaulting off towards the hidden Polymorphs.

The old man hit the ground just as Sparrow and his companions were struggling to their feet, and the shock of his landing was, if anything, greater than the dragon's; they were flung down again as if there had been an earthquake. They got back to their feet a second time, by now plastered with mud. They huddled together silently, shifting uneasily in the glare of the dragon's eye, just beyond the far corner of the cottage. Everything had gone very quiet, apart from the rushing of the stream.

Then the three Polymorphs appeared again. They came one by one, half flapping, half hopping over the lower end of the dragon's tail, and up towards the cottage. There was little menace in them now; there was something about their flapping and hopping that was a little like the capering of crows on a wheatfield. Puckel, waving the stick, appeared close behind them.

For all that, when the Polymorphs came to a stop not far away, there was nothing pleasant or amusing about them. Everyone could see them now in their proper shapes, winged and hunched at the shoulder, with their heads sticking forwards on long necks. They were not quite solid, though you couldn't actually see through them, except for a little at the edges. Their wings and the rags that hung on their bodies were grey. Their faces – which were almost human, except that they had a glistening, sagging look like newly-cooled candlewax – were grey and expressionless under the huge, domed foreheads. The small, black eyes of Ur and Eych were fixed on the ground. Only one of Bur's eyes – the silver-white one – was open. The head with the closed eye was wobbling and knocking against the other as though it were asleep. The Polymorphs were a drab, dreary sight, particularly with the green and gold magnificence of the dragon in the background, stretched like a battlemented wall across the garden, with streaks of smoke blowing along its flanks as it breathed.

"Well, a bath wouldn't do you lot any harm," said Puckel, coming up behind and looking askance at Sparrow and his friends. "That's hardly the way to look when you're meeting your neighbours for the first time – particularly you, young fellow."

Sparrow smiled weakly. Now that all the excitement seemed to be over, he was feeling distinctly trembly. What did Puckel mean by "neighbours"?

"Don't think it's all over," the old man said. "Not by any means. I'm not going to do all your work for you. I'm simply going to introduce you to your friends here and show you what we can do to help them."

"Help them?" Sparrow repeated, amazed.

"All in a manner of speaking," Puckel said,

giving him a sidelong glance, almost like a bird. "Well done, by the way," he went on. "You came through. I knew you would of course, though it had to be done."

"What had to be done? What have I come through?" Sparrow asked. The worst thing about Puckel was that the more things got themselves sorted out, the more complicated they seemed to become.

"You were told a severe test was coming to you," Puckel said. "That was it. You came through."

"I never did anything," Sparrow said.

"You guessed the dragon's name, didn't you?"

"Not really," Sparrow said. "It was just an accident. The Polymorphs' names just – got knocked together... It was just...." And then Sparrow went quiet, because he suddenly thought about the strangeness of the little Puckel-messenger. Was this another thing about himself he didn't know?

"That's right," said Puckel, who seemed to know what Sparrow was thinking. "You know more than you think you know. You're stronger than you think you are, as I said to you once before. Six names to make one name – not easy to get the order right first time, but you did, without even trying. You're the one we've been waiting for. Now put the dragon to bed."

"What?" said Sparrow.

Puckel had already turned away from him, and was starting to drive the Polymorphs closer to the door of the cottage. "I'd advise you to start at the tail," he said over his shoulder, "it's the cooler end."

Sparrow gaped after the old man, who was ushering the three Polymorphs into the cottage. He turned to the others. "What am I supposed to do now?" he said.

Gogs looked at Murie. Murie looked at Gogs. "You'd better do what he says," Kittel said.

"Thanks," said Sparrow. And because there seemed to be nothing else for it, he turned from them and walked, slithering in the mud, down through the vegetable patch, into the mown hay, towards the dragon's tail.

He reached it and stood, at a loss. Puckel's order had seemed impossible before; now it seemed just silly. The dragon stretched before him like a small hill. You couldn't move a dragon! Here, where the vast stretch of the beast tapered to its thinnest, the very end of its tail was still thicker than Sparrow's body. "Ureychyoburenitho," he murmured, fearful, yet marvelling to be so near the terrible creature. "Ureychyoburenitho." He noticed that the green and golden scales that covered the huge body were strangely delicate, each beautifully shaped, like the petal of a flower. At the very end of the tail the scales disappeared under plastered mud.

In fact the very end of the tail was buried under the mud. And just as he realized that he might actually be standing on it, the ground moved under Sparrow's feet, and the mud steamed and slipped away off the blade-like tip. Sparrow tried to step back, but the rising tail threw him forward so that he fell on the scales he had just been looking at. They felt cold – so how was it that the mud was steaming? Steam, or mist rather, seemed to be everywhere, pouring upwards, enveloping the dragon, which rapidly became a humped island of mist in a broader sea of mist all around . . .

Everything was becoming very confused. Sparrow seemed to be turning. He saw the sun appearing up on his left, a ball of dull orange fading into the deepening gloom of mist. The dragon no longer seemed to be stretched out across the ground. Its shape was now marked by a great grey coil, a vast misty spiral that boiled and billowed yet was never lost in the rolling mist that covered everything. Sparrow was moving rapidly along a road of mist, towards its centre, which he now knew was the dragon's head. Somewhere within the circle of the coils, a little below him, he saw Kittel, Murie, Gogs, Lissie and Ormand; some- where on the edge he could see Puckel and the three Polymorphs, all of them standing in the formless mist with nothing else round them; and on the other side of Puckel, on the outside of the circle, there was Bull, and three more Polymorphs lying at his feet. Sparrow was floating, circling round and round them all.

And now Puckel seemed to have picked up a thin end of the road of mist and passed it over to Bull, who was winding it round the three Polymorphs lying on the ground. Or was it the rope?

Then the coils of mist grew suddenly tight, and the edges of the circle were pulled in towards the centre, and the centre was where Sparrow stood. Puckel was right next to him. The mist was thicker than ever, but now it smelled like smoke. There was a vague whirring noise going on all this time. Puckel wheeled round towards the nearest of the Polymorphs – Ur or Eych, Sparrow couldn't tell which – seized its head, and with one almighty twist pulled it right off. "Now," the old man said in his most matter-of-fact voice, "that's one." And he threw the head down in the mist between Sparrow's feet, where it disappeared. A second later there came a dull thud from somewhere below. The Polymorph's body had meanwhile disintegrated into a small white heap, like fragments of burned bones.

Sparrow watched, rooted with shock, as Puckel proceeded to dispose of Bur's two heads, and the single head of the remaining Polymorph.

"Now you," he said, pointing a finger at Sparrow.

It was then that Sparrow saw the other three Polymorphs which had been lying at Bull's feet. They were still lying there, but things seemed to have got twisted round in a peculiar way so that they were now lying with their heads at Sparrow's feet. And it was no longer exactly three Polymorphs, because Sparrow's ordinary eye told him that he was looking at two men from the village, whom he recognized – and Ms Redwall.

"Come on, you know what to do," Puckel said.

"Do I?" said Sparrow.

"Of course you do. All that's needed is for you to get on with it."

"But—"

"Butts are for holding water. Don't waste time."

Turning then, Sparrow saw Kittel and Lissie and Murie beside him, looking down in horror at the three faces at his feet. Gogs was there too, his face sickly green. "That's Cross Lurgan and Noddy Borrow," Murie said.

They saw the crossbow bolt through Ms Redwall's neck. "Are they all dead?" Kittel and Lissie exclaimed together.

"They are bound by iron and wood to the forms they took for themselves," Puckel said softly. "Let them go, Sparrow."

Sparrow gulped several times, for now he understood. "Lissie will like this more than me," he said at last. Then he bent down over Ms Redwall, crooked his elbow under her chin, seized the top of her head with his other hand, and pulled for all he was worth. And with no more effort than pulling up a cabbage, the head came off in his arms.

There was a strangled gurgle from Gogs, but Sparrow knew his friend must now be able to see the real form of what he was holding. He dropped the Polymorph's head down between his feet, and as it fell it made a dark trail through the mist. Gently it floated out of sight into darkness; but just before it disappeared, Sparrow saw it rolling an eye at him and then winking. Again there came the dull thud from below. He turned back to Cross Lurgan and Noddy Borrow, and in a moment two more Polymorph heads followed the first one.

As this was happening, Sparrow became aware that there were shadowy figures over beyond Bull. Bull had turned away towards them, and there was a voice speaking – a man's voice – almost certainly Plato Smithers.

"A young girl, a woman and two young boys are still out there," the voice was saying. "We don't know what might have happened to them by now, and they should never have been made to go, whatever any of them may have done wrong. I'm not even sure that that young lass ever did a wrong thing anyway."

"It was a fine thing, what she was doing at the school," another voice, a little fainter, called, and there was a murmur of agreement.

"We've a lot to thank this young lad for," Smithers' voice came again, and Sparrow saw a large hand being clapped on Bull's shoulder. "He's made us think about a lot of things that we'd forgotten – things that we preferred not to think about. A Trader's son, that's what he is – and a living reminder of what Traders do for our sakes. Remember Tack Hind, the lad's father."

There was another murmur of approval, but it was almost immediately interrupted by shouts of surprise and fright, and the shadowy figures started moving, surging forwards towards Bull – though breaking into mist when they reached Puckel – backwards and forwards, stooping and straightening. "She's moving! She's getting up!" Sparrow heard, then – "Look, Noddy's all right too. Come on lad, take my hand. Come on, Cross . . ."

The forms faded, Bull became faint and shadowy, and Sparrow thought he heard a woman's voice asking in high, complaining tones why were the children not at school and what was happening and why was everyone looking like a flock of frightened sheep. Then the ground – or whatever it was he was standing on – gave way under him, and he found himself hanging by the elbows to a stone thing, scrabbling and pulling himself upwards as hands reached down to grab his hands and the mist swirled and seethed in front of his eyes.

A moment later it cleared, and he found himself standing on a solid floor, the white ash of the Polymorphs at his feet and black ash of something else still hot and smoking all round amongst fire-blackened stones. The hot sun was beating down, and his friends and Puckel were on the grass just beyond the circle of scorched ground. "Where's the dragon?" he said. "What's happened?"

"Gone to ground, gone to earth," Puckel replied. "Gone to bed, where I told you to put him. Don't be surprised. You did it. You shouldn't doubt yourself so much."

Sparrow saw the large stone he had pulled himself up by, lying half buried in a heap of ash and charred wood. Or – no – there was something else there . . . He covered his right eye and stared from the darkness of his left . . . He was at the edge of a well or a pit – a five-sided pit rimmed with five huge stones. Staring in, he found himself gazing down into the baleful, uplifted eyes of Bur of the Lamps.

Bur was standing deep down below him, and the other Polymorphs, winged and in their whole shapes, stood round in what Sparrow now saw was the little torchlit chamber with the stone table and the empty tripod and, poking through the doorway from the passage outside, the blade-shaped tip of the dragon's tail.

Sparrow found out later that after he had gone down and stood on the dragon's tail in the meadow, the others had seen the great creature crawling up over the garden to the cottage, while Sparrow climbed steadily up on to its back. When the dragon reached the cottage it pushed its head through the door and the whole cottage went up in flames and smoke and collapsed. They lost sight of Sparrow in the smoke, and there was no sign of Puckel either. But the dragon continued to crawl and gradually disappeared into the burning heap. As the smoke cleared they saw Puckel calmly ripping off the Polymorphs' heads, and when they ran over to the cottage – all except Ormand, who had fainted – they discovered Sparrow about to pull off the heads of the three villagers, after which he seemed to stumble, slipping under the great stone doorframe, which the dragon had flattened as it pushed its way in.

"The spiral of the right hand and the spiral of the left hand," Puckel remarked quietly, as he gently stroked the head of his stick. "Now this is truly the Star Wheel again, and the haunt of dragons."

"The spiral," Sparrow echoed; and those of them who had been in the maze of the

Polymorphs thought of the great body coiled round and round in its silent corridors, snug as a hand in a glove. "Is this where the dragon came from, long ago, before it got away?"

"How do you think the torches stayed alight?" Puckel snapped. "Electricity?" He was fumbling with the brooch of his midnight cloak. With an irritable grunt he tore the fastening and let the garment fall to the ground, leaving the Puckel whom Sparrow and Kittel had always known, clad in an old moss-green thing that was more tatters and patches than coat. "Phew!" he grouched. "That's better. Thought I was going to turn to butterfat in that stupid clobber.

"There is a change," he went on, "but we're none the worse for that. The dragon faces outwards now. Before, his head was to the centre. What comes of that we shall see in due course.

"Things are not finished yet, not by any means; and you haven't seen the last of that lot – " he nodded towards the hidden pit – 'so you'd better get used to the idea of them."

"Haven't you got them under control yet?" Sparrow asked.

Puckel looked at him sharply. "I have, but you haven't. And you're going to have to, though to be sure you're well on the way already. But that trick with your eyes is just the beginning, to help you to see through their nonsense. You'll have to master the Secret Way and I'd better tell you right now that that means ruling the Polymorphs stricter than a carter rules his team of horses. A lot stricter in fact; it doesn't pay to be good to them, and you should never thank them. They need a firm hand and no respect. Use them – that's all they're good for. That way they'll take you both far and fast – faster than thought."

"Where will they take me?" Sparrow asked.

"Oh, here and there. Where that idiot crow stands on your father's chest in the Vault of the Bear and says his words for him, for example."

There was a small gasp of surprise from Murie at these words, but Puckel went on – "And through all the angles of the Enclosure, and through all the nine hundred and ninety-nine doorways in the great door. You'll find out – you'll have to, if you want to find what this one's looking for." He nodded at Kittel.

"Her way home?" Sparrow said.

"Well," Puckel chuckled, "maybe her way home's not quite the way you all think it is. However, that's all one. It's time you made your way to where you think your home is for the moment. And it's not here, and that's for sure."

And without another word, Puckel vanished from their sight. Only Sparrow, just for the briefest glimpse of his left eye, saw the old man leap into the pit of the Star Wheel and disappear in a whirring and whirling of great wings. All that was left of him was a mist of dark blue forget-me-nots in the grass, where his cloak had fallen. And all that was left of the little cottage that had been their home for a fortnight was a pile of fire-blackened stones.

"Well," said Sparrow, "it is time we started back home. I've an idea they'll be glad to see us again."